A
REAL
MAN

Also by Shylah Boyd
American Made, a novel

and as Frances Whyatt
American Gypsy, poetry
Equal Time (editor)

A REAL MAN

& OTHER STORIES

BY SHYLAH BOYD

BRITISH AMERICAN PUBLISHING, LTD.

The author is indebted to The Writers Room in New York City where much of this book was written.

Clean and Gentle Moments received the P.E.N. Syndicated Fiction Award.

This novel is a work of fiction. Names, characters, places and incidents either are the product of the author's imagination or are used fictitiously. Any resemblance to actual events or locales or persons, living or dead, is entirely coincidental.

Copyright 1990 by Shylah Boyd
All rights reserved
including the right of reproduction
in whole or in part in any form
British American Publishing
3 Cornell Road
Latham, New York 12110
Manufactured in the United States of America

94 93 92 91 90 5 4 3 2 1

Library of Congress Cataloging-in-Publication Data

Boyd, Shylah.
    A real man & other stories / Shylah Boyd.
       p. cm.
    ISBN 0-945167-27-X
    I. Title.   II. Title : Real man and other stories.
PS3552.0879R4   1990
813'.54--dc20
                                                    89-28132
                                                        CIP

For my brothers,
Tick and Joe Grannis

CONTENTS

A REAL MAN

Cherry-Shiree

She looked like something out of a 1950s motorcycle movie. Blond cotton-candy hair, a size 12 poured into tight jeans, and beefy breasts with a long ample cleavage under the V-neck jersey, and you just knew she had a tattoo hidden somewhere inside all that. Anyhow, Faye liked her.

She liked Faye too—you could tell. She said "Sure honey, sure I got rosé, and if I don't got it here, I'll go next door—hole on a sec."

This was some bartender. Faye was the only woman customer. Six guys. The pits. A nervous coke-head who phoned his sister (who wasn't there) outside Seattle about every five minutes, and asked Faye if she was "actually *from* the Florida Keys," three times. Then you had the professional drunks who washed for one of three local restaurants in return for half a trailer and fun money. The name of the joint was the U Bet Bar.

"Shit, this rosé's little warm, hon—ice it down for you?"

"No thanks."

She wanted to talk. She saw the look in Faye's eye strangers always misjudged as compassion. Actually the look was curiosity. Anyhow—she talked.

"Yup—far as I'm concerned you can slide the whole state of California into the sea an I woun't blink an eye—except to get my kid and run, that's what I think of the whole thing—Goddamn son of a gun gets custody—a felon! You believe that—they give him custody—a felon? Hell, worst thing I ever done was shoplift—and this is no-shit shoplift— Tangee lipstick from Woolworths when I was twelve. Fifteen when I had her, see. . . ." she says with the cracked color snapshot out from her hip pocket. She had a problem getting the thing out, her pants were so tight, "Cute in't she. She is, God bless her."

"Yah, she's beautiful. What's your name?"

"Cherry-Shiree. What's yours?"

"Faye. I hate my name. You've got a great name."

"Yahh? Think? My Mom named me after a boutique in Laverne, Mississippi—some life, huh."

"Hell yes."

"So what do you do, Faye?"

"Depends. Write I guess."

"Yah you a writer? You look like a writer."

"How's that?"

"Smart. You look smart."

"You been on the Keys long, Cherry-Shiree?"

"Coupla years, you include Key West. Big man, big promises, usual story."

"Uh huh."

"Just gettin' it together, get my kid—"

"I'm sorry."

"So you married, hon?"

"Divorced, usual."

"Yah, join the human race huh. Hell, I get off in an hour, you wanna toss a few at Zips?"

"Zips? Sure. Zips."

"I'll give you some stories to write—tell you that much."

"I believe it—Zips," Faye said, and tipped her the price of the wine, then went home to feed the animals.

After she fed the dogs, the two stray cats, hers and Ralph's pet rat snake, her toucan, and Ralph's tarantula, there was thirty minutes before the ride up to Zips, so she skimmed the pool, called Mike the mechanic to ask about her ailing BMW, and read the *Sunday Book Review*. Then she took Ralph's Porsche out and said the hell with the loaner.

Cherry-Shiree was already at Zips, though Faye was a couple of minutes early. A greaser was buying her drinks—another guy standing behind, had his eyes down her jersey. The place was a jumble of dope smugglers, college kids, and Moms and Pops for Saturday night rum and cokes.

"Hey."

"Hey Faye. Meet the guys."

She met the guys. They exuded that kind of oily politeness like they'd been told she was not just a 'nuther dumb cunt'.

"Yah we already knowed who you were—din't we, Cherry-Shiree. . . ."

"Yup, God's truth, Faye—whatcha drinkin'?"

"Coke."

"Coke?"

"Yah, Coke."

"Honey, coke's somethin' you put up your nose."

"Oh yah . . . nose huh. . . . No, seriously—Coca-cola's fine."

"Faye here's my new friend, guys. Hey, Don, show her how you make an elephant disappear."

Don, who was tall, thin except for his gut, and sported a greasy black Prince Valiant, leaned towards Faye.

"Oh yah," she said, "that's how you make an elephant disappear?" Faye was sorry she'd come.

"Wanna see how I make the elephant come back?"

"Not on one Coca-cola. That was truly spectacular, Don."

Cherry-Shiree said as how her and Faye had girl-talk to make and whyn't they excuse them for a minute—they'd be right back.

Upstairs at Zips the Tahitian girl was doing her rope dance with the tourists and there were children around. Downstairs was "local" and where the boats pulled in. Downstairs was also known as the Free Fire Zone.

"Listen, I did a lot of things in my life, but never for money. You do it for money, it changes you."

"Sounds right to me. . . ."

". . . See I figure, anything I do bad'll reflect on my kid and I want her. I want my baby."

Cherry-Shiree pointed to one of the big Magnum boats docked by itself at the end of the longest pier. "That other guy, Rick? That's his—said how'd I like to make ten thou—all I need is a driver's license . . . follow me?"

"Sure."

"Ten thou'd buy my kid back from that bastard. He don't love her—he's got her but he don't really love her. Guy can't love shit, man. Hey, right now I need a friend—I don't need no one-night thing and I don't need a lot of booze. . . ." she said, looking over at Faye, as straight in the eye as she could since Faye figured she'd already done something, and her eyes had that wine-stain coloring around the retinas. "Look, I trust you, Faye—you meet someone once a blue moon you trust even though you don't know shit about them. So I know you'll tell me what I should do, and it'll be all right if I do it."

"I don't know what you should do, Cherry-Shiree. All I can do is maybe help you see things the way they are—that's the best friends can do I think. . . ."

"Hey . . . SEE, you're already helping—you know how to make things clear—see if I got the ten thou and I went back to California and just said, 'hey, you take the ten grand and I'll take the kid'—if I got the ten that is—I mean, what would you do?"

"If I were you?"

"Yah, if you were me, and you could think like you—wanna drink?"

"Now I do—I'll treat," Faye said and ordered herself a Bacardi Anejo on the rocks, Cherry-Shiree a Canadian Mist and Seven-up. The Tahitian dancer had taken a break because of the sunset. It was one of the better ones this time, lots of thunderheads and red and orange covering the water. "Wellll," she said after the first sip, the Anejo burning a little, "Well, what I think you have to consider is the law of probabilities here—the first probability is whether or not they'd actually pay you your ten thousand. I'd say that's doubtful, and it's probably dangerous. Then, even if you got the money, you don't know how your ex-husband would react. Here you go all the way back to California and he's moved, or has an unlisted number, and maybe you find him and he takes your money but doesn't give you your daughter. Then again you could steal your daughter and go live somewhere in hiding—you could try that—but see, you stand out, Cherry-Shiree—people see you fast, the way you look. . . ."

"You think I look like a pro, Faye?"

"I don't know. I saw some pro's in Amsterdam once who looked like they taught sixth grade, so I don't know. Let's just say you're provocative. Listen, you want to come back to my house? We can talk better."

"Sure. Who needs those creeps."

So Faye took her back. She hadn't the foggiest why. She didn't know why she'd more or less picked up this bleached blond person or why she'd agreed to Zips or why she was thinking of a plan. Driving down the four-mile strip—then the Old Road—then opening the gate which was half-hidden to the double lot with the trees making a jungle of it and the two-story house with the verandas full round, the pool, the Spanish chairs, and carved oak bed—the whole nut of the advance she and Ralph had gotten on the movie—throwing it in her face—only Cherry-Shiree had the kid and Faye didn't and wouldn't and maybe couldn't without some fancy procedure she was going to go through anyway—maybe that was what Cherry-Shiree'd call the bottom line. And Ralph'd been gone for a week. Maybe a week. Maybe forever.

"My God," Cherry-Shiree kept saying. "My God!" Both of them floating in the pool naked with the moon at quarter wane overhead and that pitch with all the stars. "I guess if I didn't like you so much, I'd sure hate your guts."

"It's not what you think. By the way, my animals like you—they don't like that many people. You're very kind to animals aren't you, Cherry-Shiree?"

"Oh yah—even throw bugs out stead of squashing them— you believe that?" She smiled with her poufed hair flat and wet down her back, and her mascara streaked. She looked younger. "You always live here?"

"No. I've lived here four years. Before that I lived in France."

"Paris, France?"

"No. A small village right above the coast," handing her a towel. It struck Faye, the pink skin—like Monroe was said to have had, that luminescent pink skin.

"You gotta boyfriend, right?"

"I did. I may still have. I'm not sure—"

"But no kids."

"No. No kids."

"You want kids?"

"Who knows. Anyway, it's unlikely I can, at least not without going through this procedure, so. . . ."

"Yah—I don't know why I figured that—but I figured that. Well, it isn't glory, that's for sure."

"No. Nothing is. Even this isn't. But I think you could get your daughter back if you want. I think you could do that."

They were sitting on the veranda. Faye had grilled the fish caught earlier and filleted by her day-worker. It was good mahi-mahi with a lime sauce. She made a green salad and poured her some of last night's pouilly fumé. Cherry-Shiree made a face at first, then said she liked it. Faye drank Coke.

"How could I?"

"Write down all the information you have on your ex-husband and daughter."

She handed her the legal pad and pencil, and while Cherry-

Shiree wrote, cleared away the dishes. When Faye came back, she'd finished.

"Okay, now what?"

"Now, I make a phone call."

Faye called the lawyer in California who'd said "I owe you one" a couple of times and who'd made a considerable sum off of two movie deals with Faye and Ralph. She told him she didn't understand how you do these things, but to do it. He said he'd just gotten back from a party with the Oscar nominees and it was a crashing bore, and it made him feel a lot better to hear Faye sounding so well.

"My lawyer's going to get on it," she said while Cherry-Shiree played with her hair at the bedroom mirror.

"I always wanted a canopy bed when I was a kid." She turned around, smiled. The blue jeans seemed looser.

"So did I. That's why I have one now . . . listen, Cherry-Shiree, don't do your hair."

"Why?"

"You need to change your image. It'd help. It'll make or break you through the system. And at least until you get your daughter back."

"But then I won't be myself."

"Yah you will. Just be in disguise for a while then. Can you do that? And you should get some community credentials—church or something. And stop working as a bartender—particularly where you are now."

"Just like that? I can't."

"Can you type?"

"Nuh uh. Quit school in the ninth grade."

"Can you clean house? Shop? Domestic stuff?"

"Oh sure."

"Well, you can work here. You can do all the house shopping, and clean five days a week, and take care of the animals—see this. . . ." Faye brought out a shirtwaist cotton dress Ralph's mother had forgotten to take back with her.

"Put it on, and I'll do your hair—come on, this is a dry run—what have you got to lose?"

"And this'll get her back and then I can be myself again?"

"Yup."

"Maybe I shouldn't be exactly myself again—Hey, you know what—I always got religion—shit, I'm always prayin' and I'm a lot nicer than some of those bitches who just pretend."

"Yes, you are. Will you do it?"

"Yah. Yah, I'll do it."

Six months later, Cherry-Shiree got her daughter back. She was a terrible housekeeper, but good with the animals. The whole deal cost Faye ten thousand dollars—four for her, four for the father, and two for the paperwork; the lawyer was a freebee. Now Faye gets letters from Mazoula, Montana, with pentecostal pamphlets, and snapshots of her newborn, Faye Hope Charity Ruskin—and her husband the Reverend Charles Ruskin—and her older daughter, Letitia.

But Ralph and Faye were quits like she thought.

Concerning God
and Pirates

Faye used to dive this wreck off Alligator Light. When she and Ralph were living together they came out here maybe once a month. It was only in twenty feet of water, which was some of the greenest water around owing to its coral bottom and no sea plants around. And it wasn't much of a wreck, only the remains of a small eighteenth-century galleon long since picked clean except for the ballast balls and an occasional doubloon if you were lucky. But it was near, only about a mile out of Lower Matecumbe Key, and easy and safe for her in the Boston Whaler.

Safety was a big thing down here, when you were out in a skiff alone, especially a woman. What with the dope smugglers and low-life types, plus she wasn't much on engines. If something major went wrong, she'd just have to sit it out. So generally she stayed in close and didn't go out in the back-country by herself unless she was mad enough or wanted to prove something. Here you could still see the outline of Long Key and Lower Matecumbe, and you were just off a flat so if the weather blew up quickly or a waterspout got you . . . you could get over to where the water was one or two feet deep and wait for the Marine Patrol.

She went down and brought up two balls. It was only around eleven and Tuesday was a slow day with all the tourists gone on Monday, and the weather was fine, nice sun, a few high clouds, not too hot, and just enough of a breeze to cool her skin but not so as to put a chop on the water.

On the second pass around the hull she started thinking about last year again. . . . What she couldn't get out of her head—about the departure of Ralph, and having her house broken into a week later . . . about being burned out on the Keys, which were beginning to look like Ft. Lauderdale South and feel like Cartagena, and being fed up and paranoid in general and being burned out on the extent of her own loneliness. Mostly it was the loneliness. That, and she was restless. She had this feeling—if she could somehow take her car and a pup tent and just go West, everything would come together. It'd be new, and pristine, and uncluttered. But not now. Now—today—it was too beautiful out here to think about anything.

She'd had it with the diving for awhile, and cracked the Lancers and took up her binoculars to watch the bird action on the far flat. It took a minute to get the focus right and when she did, thinking she was spotting an especially big heron, saw that it was instead a bald eagle. Now that *was* something. You saw them but not frequently and half the time you thought you saw one, it turned out to be an osprey or what they called sea hawk, which abound around here and build their nests the size of condos on top of all those telephone poles running down Highway One and from just south of the 18-mile stretch all the way to Boca Cheeca. She made note of the eagle in her journal, and followed the line of pelicans and herons feeding off the same place on the flat. She thought maybe a big shark had washed up, and after some of the Lancers felt of a mind to go over and investigate.

It was pretty bad what she saw. Real bad. You don't know what salt water and heat does until you see a body that way. Like some gigantic carp with the features dissolved and predators had gouged out the rest. It was pretty bad. But she had no reaction other than a fleeting one of being scared. This was after she'd put the motor on tilt and poled her way to the center of the flat which took some time in the doing and she figured she'd better get back and report it quickly . . . so it was maybe forty-five minutes or maybe it was an hour before she got back out into deep water and set the engine down, and pulled up the choke. But it wouldn't start. You could hear it trying, but it wouldn't kick over. So for a while she kept trying and then stopping to pause so it wouldn't flood, but it didn't go.

She got out the manual and put the engine back on tilt, and took off the lid. Then she backtracked and pumped the gas in case there was a drag on it, but that didn't work, and she fiddled around with a screwdriver tightening a loose bolt, but couldn't find anything. So then she put it down and tried to hand-start it, but that didn't work, and it just seemed typical that everything got screwed up at once including the weather, because she saw the squall line moving up.

By this time she was wavering between a sort of testy calm and fear, and she'd tried to hail one of the guides going out the channel, but he was too far away, so there was nothing to do but stay at the edge of the flat until help came, meaning any boat passing.

It was deader than usual. Normally she would have seen even on a slow day half a dozen skiffs go by, but it'd been an hour of nothing other than the guide who didn't see her. So she sat and finished off the Lancers and smoked and tinkered some more with the engine, then put her mask down to the water and watched the action. There wasn't much. A bull shark passing in the deep part of the channel, a school of small snappers. One large conch shell she considered diving for, but the shark around put her off. So she stayed in the boat and waited, watching the squall move in, and tried not to think about the body.

"Heyheyhey. Y'all got some trouble I see."

"Engine won't start."

"No kidding."

"Right."

"We'll gitcha out okay."

"Listen, there's a body on that flat."

"A body?"

"Yes, a human body."

"No kidding."

"No kidding."

This couldn't be happening. There was no way this could be happening, and by now the squall was full on so she was soaking and bailing the boat. There were four men in what she guessed to be a 24-footer—wide-hulled, looked new, and every one of the dudes looked like he'd just done in his mother, and she wanted to scream "please don't help me," but it was too late and if she hadn't been such an idiot and just anchored the Whaler on the flat, she could have swam it to shore before then, given half the distance was flats, and there weren't too many sharks and no real current. So now what should she do, and maybe she shouldn't have told them about the body, but it just came out, and the hard rain made it impossible to see.

"Listen, get on the boat, we'll take y'all in."

"No. That's okay. I'll fix it."

"You can't fix it, honey . . . hey Joe, she thinks she can fix it."

"Hey, you think you can fix it. How 'bout we tow it."

"No. That's okay."

"Well, we're gonna tow it, y'all jus' get on the boat." Which was when the big one with the scar on his neck, the one called Joe, got in the Whaler and got her by the upper arms.

"Hey, we got us a lahve one."

"No please. Please don't."

"Please don't what."

"I'll get it fixed. You guys go on."

"Damn, we done got ourselves a lahve one."

They must've knocked her silly because the next thing she knew she was in the cabin, and they were already past the Channel Two Bridge on the other side in the Bay, and it was peculiar how clear-headed she was despite what was happening and the fact her head hurt worse than she could imagine, and despite her knowing the program because what else was it. Four men, white boys with white trash written all over and maybe they were smugglers and maybe not— maybe just pirates who could fix and use her boat once they got out between the mangroves far away enough, and she kept her eyes to a slit because the one called Joe was in the cabin watching her and with her eyes like that she figured she was better off than with them open. She figured they'd want her awake. So she waited until Joe went above and then she looked around and didn't see anything except that she was lying on a bunk opposite the table, and she knew enough to think beyond right now.

There weren't any guns around loose that she could see. She figured what they didn't have in the cockpit would be in the hold. And there was no way she could squeeze out of the porthole, if you called it that—actually double windows with a slide, but still too small. She rose up high enough to check the table and galley top. A lot of little baggies on the table with pills in them. Six or seven different kinds she didn't recognize—two she did. The red capsules and white tablets. At least she thought so. And the galley had a half a liter full of dark rum, which was good because the dark had a more full-bodied taste and maybe would mask the taste of the pills, and she had to gamble she could do it without them coming down, and that they'd finish the rum, which she figured they would because they smelled of it already, so if she did it now, it was all she could do.

The thing was to make her motions fluid and get down low. So she got down low and reached up on the table for the two baggies. And the hope was they'd keep talking and laughing and still at speed. She couldn't gauge how long it'd take or if she could even do it, she just did it, lying on her stomach and then reaching up for the rum. Bringing herself up high enough to get at the bottle in the galley. Then she opened the baggies, and took maybe twenty of each, maybe it was more—about a quarter of what was in each baggie—and unscrewed the lid. Then she figured she didn't have a prayer on account of having to open the capsules one at a time and pour the contents in—the tablets she probably could partially pulverize in one of the loose baggies, and she did that first, and that worked—and she put it in the rum. Then she started doing the capsules, in the same baggie—one at a time but faster than she thought she could. All the while on her stomach because she figured even though the risk was greater she'd save time rather than getting back on the bunk. And they were still talking. But going slower now and that was bad, assuming it'd take twenty minutes for the stuff to take effect anyway. It really wasn't a very workable plan. But she finished it all the same—taking maybe fifteen minutes to get it all in the rum, wipe the lip off, twist the cap back on, shake it hard for a couple of minutes and get back on the bunk.

Her head was in pretty bad shape and she felt the clot of blood with her fingers, then put her hand down fast when Joe came back.

"Hey Sam, she still out."

"Nah. I din't hit her hard."

"Yah. She out cold, maybe we dust her, have li'le fun first."

"Wait til we get where I tole you."

"Man, she droolin'. That mean she gonna die—lahk foam?"

"Oh mannnn, how I know?"

"I wan her live for it, man I ain't no sicko."

"Get that rum an shut-up."

"She ain't no chicken."

"No, but she ain't bad."

"Nahce stuff."

"Naw. Too li'le."

"Hey jus' bring the rum, man."

She figured there was a chance he'd touch her, get that close, and she never did once think about what she was going to do, she just did things on instinct. Like getting the saliva up in her mouth and making it form bubbles and lay around her lips and chin, and she bit hard down on her tongue—she never could have done that if she'd been thinking—take a chunk of her tongue out so there'd be blood with the spit—make him think maybe she'd hemorrhaged. And when he yanked at the top of her suit and pinched her she'd been ready and held her breath, and just bit into the flesh of her tongue and kept telling herself it was only pain. You could fix pain.

Joe went back with the rum, and they sped up again, and she figured by now they were way out in the backcountry water. Maybe they were drinking the rum and maybe not, and she didn't know if they could taste the difference, so she lay there with her eyes open and crying because of the pain to her tongue. She couldn't get a fix on time but it seemed long, and she had time enough to think maybe she was in shock.

They slowed up again, and she could tell this time they were easing through a channel between islands because she could hear the whoosh of the mangrove branches against the ch3 hull. So then she could hear them again, even though they kept the engine on.

"Goddamn am I drunk. Hey you drunk?"

"Yah. Don't thin . . . don't . . . don. . . ."

"Can't cut—not drun. . . ."

"Drushed us. . . ."

"Dushed, cun done . . . goin down fo. . . ."

"Hel muh yuh fuggrrrs. . . ."

In the back of her mind she figured it might be an act, so she waited a long time or it seemed that way until she worked up the guts to check the window of the hatch, and saw two of them laid out on deck but she still didn't quite believe it. Although if they weren't, she was dead anyway. So she went out and saw the empty liter rolling towards the stern, and Joe face down in the water—the other three were out, and she thought about trying to put them face down in the water too—for insurance maybe, or for what reason she wasn't sure—but then decided not, and worked on freeing her boat which they'd double-tied to the stern.

When all of it was done—the untying of the double bowline, pulling herself over the side and into the Whaler—that was the first time she prayed after all the things she could have prayed for. She prayed they wouldn't come to, she prayed the engine would start—all the while she was babying the choke up and checking to see it was in neutral and pumping the tanks. Which it did, the first try. Started strong—too strong because she still had the choke up, but eased it back so slowly it seemed to take minutes before she put it in gear and eased out from behind the stern of the bigger boat and got clear of the mangroves.

For awhile she was lost and kept looking for land or Rabbit Key as a kind of marker, taking the Whaler on a due northeast. It was all sixth sense and guess because out here with the mangrove islands all looking the same and without point of land it could drive you dizzy. Then she saw the top of Seminole Tower and the radio booster through the binoculars, and by the light she figured it was around six. She was hurting badly, hurting and crying and taking the channel full open. And she knew when she got back to the marina where she kept the Whaler, it'd already be closed up and everyone off at the Tiki Bar. No one around to help her if she passed out.

So then the light had begun to turn that peach apricot it does before an April sunset and the water was dead still, and she was the only one through, making the fast cut before the channel opened up for the marina—and it hit her. It hit

her all at once. What had happened. The body on the flat.
How it looked. And the boat starting as it did when before
it wouldn't. And how the pills worked. What chance was
that? Maybe one in fifty, the pills in the rum would work.
And if they worked, it meant they were all dead. The one,
Joe, she knew was dead. He had to be dead with his face
down in the water, but then she figured he hadn't drowned
because he was floating, although maybe it was the high salt
content that kept him that way. So figure they were all dead.
Or maybe they weren't dead. Not then. Maybe they weren't
dead. But would die. Or maybe she was crazy. But she wasn't.
She'd bit a chunk of her tongue off and her head hurt. And
when she got the boat tied securely to the pilings, and got
her gear on the dock, she wasn't sure what she should do.
Get the cops. She knew she had to get to a hospital. She
figured she was in shock, or maybe it had driven her crazy.
And she was shaking all over. Cold. But she could still look
at the sunset, and see it for what it was, and the roseate
spoonbills feeding off the chum at the edge of the flat, and
how elegant they were.

A Bum and
His Money

Faye watched the old derelict with his hair down to
his shoulders and the filthy bandanna triple-knotted around
his forehead and his belly as big and hard as a woman in
her eighth month get into a taxi on Collins Avenue. It was
hot—a fry-an-egg-on-the-sidewalk swelter as the DJs call it.
You could see the sweat dripping off his nose, the red eyes
swollen half-shut with crud between the lashes—then what
he does is reach into his pocket and take out this fistful of
tens. It was some sight.

She was getting on the bus when she saw the cab driver
pick him up, and it occurred to her the cabbie might roll
him, maybe take him off I-95 and kill him for the money.
This happened in less than five minutes, and whether it was
the bizarre nature of the occurrence (the cab driver was as
seedy-looking as the bum) or just her paranoia being in Miami,
Faye stepped down from the first rung and wrote out the
number of the cab.

When she dialed 911, the receiving cop thought she was
nuts, but he didn't say as much. What he said was . . .
"Well hon, you're not telling me that any specific illegal act
is being perpetrated."

"Yes, but I've got a hunch about it. It looked wrong."

"A hunch, uh huh, a hunch." But he took the number
and the descriptions, and said he'd put the number out,

which Faye only half-believed. . . . Anyway she felt she'd
done what she could, and decided to walk instead of take
the bus.

The heat was incredible, 99 degrees which is not so record-
breaking but down here it felt like 130. You could see those
wavy emanations of swelter coming off the hotels jammed
one blond monolith beside the next, their doormen leaning
on railings and not opening car doors anymore but staring
out at the iridescence in their fancy uniforms—and the elderly
Jewish couples that in more temperate weather walked cheerfully arm-in-arm, cane-in-cane, stopping now at park benches.

"That was good what you did, Miss. . . . I woulda done
it myself."

"Yes. That didn't look right to us."

They had been in line behind Faye on the bus, but now
sat up aways on one of the benches.

"We got off, too. It didn't look kosher, did it, Mort. You
did a good thing, Miss."

"Well, I just had a hunch."

"He should be in a hospital. Terrible that stomach."

"Yes, he should."

"Wonder how come he was here."

"He stood out."

"Well, it's good to be careful."

Faye asked if she might help them into the air-conditioned
lobby of the Americana, which was the closest hotel, but
they were afraid—it was way over budget. Faye said she
didn't think they need buy anything just to sit in the cool
air, but they were pensioners and she saw it made them
nervous. She said she thought the heat was dangerous, and
the woman, whose name was Rose, said as how Mort was
asthmatic, but even so—they'd wait for the next bus. The
bus pulled up and it was crowded, and the air-conditioning
didn't work. Faye watched them start to get on, then get
off again.

"Where do you folks live?"

They mentioned a cheap stucco place she knew in the Art
Deco section about six miles down the strip.

"I have a car parked nearby. I was just taking the bus to
avoid the hassle. Let me give you a ride. It won't be any
trouble."

"Oh no. We couldn't."

"Really, I might as well. I've decided to drive it anyway."

"Well, if it's no trouble."

"No trouble, really."

In the car they talked about crime and hot weather, and
gave off a muskiness of old age and perfumed lotions. . . .
They said they'd been married ten years, which probably
meant they married in their seventies. . . . They said it was
a first marriage, and Rose giggled when Mort added they
had no children between them.

"We gotta good thing going. Haven't we got a good thing
going, Rose?"

"What?"

"I said we gotta good marriage, huh Rose. She's a little
hard of hearing in her left ear."

"I hear you. That cab driver. . . ."

"Yes. . . ."

". . . didn't look kosher."

"No, he looked like a gypsy."

"You think he was a gypsy?"

"He had a hoop in his ear."

"Really. I didn't notice."

"Where'd he get so much money?"

"Hard to say. He might have stolen it."

"No, he was a sick man."

"Yes, he looked it."

"He should be in a hospital."

"Funny to see an old bum on Collins Avenue."

"Yes. You never used to."

"No."

"But now you see anything."

"Yes."

"The crime and sick people."

"Yes, it's a shame."

They were going up the stone pathway to their villa-lette with Faye in the middle and them hanging on to her arms so that they could both use their canes on the outside. It was the heat, not their age. Faye could tell Mort was rationing his breath. Inside, it felt like a meat locker, probably 65 degrees but after the humidity it seemed colder. The name-plate on the little plastic knocker was Feinstein.

"You any relation to Keekee Feinstein?"

"Keekee! Keekee's my niece. You know her?"

"I met her at a health spa. We became friends."

"She's a good girl. She doesn't weigh 200 pounds anymore."

"That's wonderful. She kept it off."

"She's a wonderful girl. So smart."

"She still head of that hotel?"

"Whole chain of'm now."

Rose talked a little about Keekee, while Faye turned the air-conditioner down to medium cool, but then Mort got back to the old bum.

"You hear anything about him. You let us know?"

He gave Faye their telephone number at the door. She said it was a privilege meeting a happily married couple in this day and age.

Back in the car, the traffic was coming up on rush hour. . . . Faye managed I-95 after a back-up behind an overheating van and fished into the speed lane—then once free of the Beach, angled down to the Palmetto Expressway . . . past the bumper-to-bumper of Miami International, until she could get on the Turnpike Extension South, which was clear sailing past Coral Gables—heading towards Florida City and the Keys.

Over the Homestead Redlands a large thunderhead was building—meaning a break in the temperature around the time Faye made it to Key Largo. She switched on the radio for the news, which mostly concerned itself with the 102-degree record set an hour ago. The edge of the Glades shimmered gold and the sky was that hard, cloudless cobalt except for the thunderhead over the Redlands twenty miles south.

Mort and Rose Feinstein were by now finishing up their salami sandwiches and camomile iced tea. What they'd offered and she'd refused—for reasons she wasn't even sure of—their poverty maybe or her own shyness—when Faye saw the camp numbers on her forearm, that overwhelmed her. But it had been a pleasant interlude after the old bum and the gypsy cab driver . . . meeting them—being able to be of service, exchanging simple kindnesses. If there was some other thing going on—she wasn't sure. Gentleness maybe, or the survival of it. Like, she thought, the villa-lette, filled with their personalities. Rose's lace doilies on the vinyl sofa, pictures from Poland, a small dented samovar polished to a high shine, his golf clubs—but he said he no longer played. A fancy card table with a deck set-up and chips. They played canasta and mah-jongg a lot. Dominoes, checkers. A portable oxygen unit in the corner. A homemade babka under a glass cover, a crocheted afghan with pinks and oranges predominating. A book on understanding Social Security. They were both retired bookkeepers. They confessed a passion for going to the greyhound races, but they only took twenty dollars between them when they went. Their sins were small, their needs limited, their health pre-eminent . . . they professed happiness.

The end of the Turnpike Extension fed into Highway One at Florida City. Faye heard the first roll of thunder in the Glades. The news reported a sharp rise in drug-associated homicides in the month of August. A guest sociologist went on to elaborate the relationship between mood-altering substances and hot weather. She turned off at Fat Dixie's for the usual beer and barbecue.

Inside, it smelled of air-conditioning mixed with barbecue

and cigarettes. The big picnic-style tables were mostly empty since it was still early to eat. Faye sat at the dark bar with the photo of Florida's fattest man eating Fat Dixie's baby back ribs and exchanged greetings with Merrilee, the day bartender, who was used to her showing up at odd hours of the afternoon.

"Headin' home, are yuh?"

"Yup. Hope it cools off."

"Keys are always ten degrees cooler."

"Yup."

"Well, howyuh doin' girl?"

"Fine, fine. Like your hair, Merrilee."

"Don't think it's too red?"

"Uh uh. Looks good."

"Usual?"

"Yup. Extra sauce."

"I got that." She pauses, "Hey, you gonna take that campin' trip you been rattlin' about?"

"Yup. Yup, I think so."

Faye looked around at the five-to-sixer's. Couple of truckers who hauled to the Keys, three locals, looked to be in their early twenties—good-looking, reasonably affluent, two gold chains apiece, and Porsche sunglasses pushed back on their heads. She vaguely knew them. One guy had been two classes behind her.

The TV announced a shootout on Alligator Alley just west of the Lauderdale exchange. Two Hispanics in a van and two unidentified men in a Miami taxi found shot in the head, execution-style . . . both vehicles discovered in three feet of water in a ditch off the highway. It appeared the cab had been firebombed. An investigation into whether it was drug-related had already gotten under way, although names were being withheld until positive identification. They showed a close shot of the rear of the cab . . . its gutted front end . . . four covered bodies on stretchers by the curb. Faye checked the numbers, but she already knew they matched. It was one of those three-number series, easy to remember.

"Whatsa matter, you look like y'all seen a ghost?"

"I saw that cab earlier."

"You what?"

"Never mind. Where's the payphone?"

"Outside, but it don't work. Is it important?"

"Well yah, I guess it is."

"Use mine. You callin' the cops or something?"

"No, this old couple I promised. It's just one of those weird occurrences. Too hard to explain."

The Hotel Ponce De Leon

The bus had collided with a tractor and broke through the railing at a point where it was deepest, and by eight that night they were still pulling bodies out—the worst the county'd seen in years despite its being a mean stretch of two-lane. It'd be morning at least before the next scheduled one, and the guy at the depot couldn't make any promises if the water level wasn't down—so you got your choice of the bus station, which'll stay open, or Shrecks Motel or the old Ponce De Leon Hotel, which don't look like much but it's clean and the food's good—what'll it be—be glad'ta phone over Miz Cheryl. . . .

"The hotel, thanks. That's it across the road?"

"Yup."

"Here now, little lady, lemme help you with that. . . ." This creep comes up to her. Goldchains—that was her name for him, the guy who sat behind her on the bus and wafted Brut—picked up her portable electric, which wasn't going anywhere for the moment anyway, and brought it towards her. "Hell, that weighs a ton. Whatcha got there?"

"Typewriter. They do have a room?"

"Yes maam, they do. Shared bath—he with you?"

"No."

"I better be doin' the same thing."

"She got rooms—you jus' go right on over."

It was already after ten—dead as a tomb in Ponce De Leon, which despite its name was a tired Central Florida farm town with everything closing down after nine except the pool parlor where she could hear the clicking balls and quarters being put up. And even with this layover for the connecting bus, which was the one that had the accident, and the incredible rain—she was wide awake, jittery about being in this place with no other women on the passenger list, jittery over an overdue article she'd sent into the magazine she knew wasn't very good, jittery and miserable she was going through the divorce and feeling the death of whatever one feels even when things don't work out—failure, or a case of the "what ifs," and jittery over the next leg of a cross-country camping trip temporarily bollixed because of a broken manifold and her having to take four buses all the way from Eustis to Daytona and back for the parts. Which didn't amount to bubkes when something really horrible occurs—like the accident.

"Here, lemme take that."

Goldchains held her typewriter and an umbrella for getting across the road which was no mean trick considering its angle and the water cascading down without any run-offs. There wasn't much she could do.

The hotel was three-story clapboard—white in need of a paint job with dark green trim, gingerbreading Southern style, and four short columns. There were two entrances—one said "registration" and next to it with a neon Miller sign in the window—Tap Room, If We Don't Like You, We Won't Serve You.

Inside, Miz Cheryl pushed out the registration form and gave her the once-over—the wet jeans and hair, boots, her height. She was one of those slightly plump, pretty-faced middle-aged women—probably wasn't ten years between the two of them, only where they'd been and how they lived, and you knew it was one of those hit-or-miss confrontations, so Faye looked her full in the eye as honestly as she could, and Miz Cheryl made up her mind.

"Jeezus girl, you look like y'all could use a drink. He with you?"

"No. He's from the bus though."

"Well, there's a ladies off the porch over there—go in and dry off while I finish doin' this. Just leave your stuff."

After she got back, with a few minutes to comb her hair and put things together, Goldchains was still hanging around, and a few others had come in from the bus depot. Miz Cheryl raised her eyebrow, looking from her to him.

"Too late for the restaurant, but we'll fix y'all something in the Tap Room—you jus' go right on in. That's my husband, Jimmy, behind the bar. Here you go, Mr. Floyd, Room One, right down this hall, first floor."

"How 'bout I buy you a steak, little lady?" Goldchains was still in there pitching.

"No thanks, I better settle in."

"Y'all gonna be upstairs hon, I better show you—Tamara!!! This is my daughter. Tamara, you finish checkin' these folks in while I take her up." Tamara smiled tentatively at Goldchains. She was around 15, short and very cute. In a couple of years, she'd be Daisy Mae.

"Pig, in't he. . . ." Cheryl said when they'd gotten to the top of the second set of stairs and she was unlocking the door, "I know the type. What they call you? Cornelia Faye's kinda formal."

"Just Faye."

She was fluffing up the spread, "Well, this the best room I got, Faye. I save it for someone I like right away."

It was a nice room, on an el—one of those cozy third floor conversions where the eaves come down like part of an envelope. Neat. Everything mismatched and handmade. Obviously, the bedspread was her pride. She told Faye she made it from one of those kits, and her niece painted the picture of the sheep. The bathroom next door had been ajaxed to a shine and was big enough to hold a wicker vanity and chest of drawers. It was clear she took pride in these things.

"I'll bet you're a writer."

"Yes."

"Make any money at it?"

"Sometimes. It's hit or miss."

"Must be real hard work. I got a cousin works on the *Miami Herald*."

"That's demanding work, working for a big newspaper."

"I'll say it is . . . he's a good boy though, always did good in school. Same age as me, forty-seven. How old're you, if you don't mind my asking."

"Forty."

"You gotta be kidding. I swear I pegged you for early thirties. . . ."

"It's the jeans and boots. . . ."

"You ever been in a flood before?"

"No. A hurricane in the Keys, that's where I'm from, but not a flood."

"It can get real bad—funny, I wouldn'a figured you for bein' from these parts."

"Well, I've lived in New York."

"Yah, I could see that. Funny, you're forty."

"Well, you don't look any older than me, do you think?" Faye and Cheryl knew it was the life did that, and they smiled at each other knowing it, and Cheryl pulled out a picture of last year's family reunion, pointed out her eight kids, the oldest being thirty-one and the youngest, the baby, six.

"That one come as a complete surprise. Jennifer, she's over at her sister's. You don't have any do you?"

"No."

"Well, yuh know, it takes you over."

"It's a whole life."

"Yup. There ain't much left over. But I wouldn't change

none of it. Lots a women I know, respectable women—
damn good mothers, too—say they got regrets, but not me.
We had some hard years, but I'd say things turned out good."

"It's a hell of an accomplishment, raising kids well, don't
you think?"

"Well, I never thought of it like that, but you could say.
I come from farm people and Jimmy do too. We had us a
hundred acre spread 'til last year. We jus' got froze out our
citrus crop one too many seasons, and Jimmy's cousin—he
and his wife had this place and they were gettin' too old—
so we figured we'd keep it in the family. Sides, to tell the
truth, I kinda like the cooking part."

"Yah me, too. I like to cook. Especially for lots of people.
It's fun."

They'd gone into the Tap Room together—a throwback
to the Fifties of Faye's girlhood, all dark with illuminated
beer signs giving a kaleidoscope off the walls, and then that
funny, kind of appealing smell of beer, smoke, peanuts, and
peanut shells.

She noticed three or four others from the bus—plus Goldchains, who was sitting at the bar. He wasn't so bad, he
could have been a lot worse. She had him down for drugs—
but everyone around here was into it—probably half the
farmers too, just in a different way. This guy looked Miami,
with too much thick, wavy hair . . . and there was something
about a man who wore his shirt open to the fourth button—
it was like a woman wearing a push-up bra under a low-cut
sundress. It branded you. Or maybe he was an accountant—
lots of Miami types dressed that way—or California types.
It was the life. And he'd been pleasant. Although Cheryl
thought the same about him as she did.

Cheryl had gone out to the kitchen, where her number-
three son was working the grill. What with the flood and
the bus layovers, it'd keep them up most the night. Faye
ordered the "king" t-bone, a double shot of Jack Daniels—
then thought what the hell why not—with a beer chaser.

It was like being eight years old in Kneepyknawk, Wisconsin again—same atmosphere as the little joint her parents always stopped at before they got over to the duck club. Instant deja vu. The wind-up clowns behind the bar that went bananas every time someone left a tip, the vinyl chairs and stools, everyone talking to each other—and outside the steady beat and damp of the rain.

"What's the latest on that bus?"

"Nine dead and another twelve they took to Deland. Be awhile before they get the full count."

"Never seen nuthin like it these parts. Not never."

"Yup. Worst ever."

"Shame, damn shame. Hell, that bridge been waitin' for an accident for years."

"Yup. County shoulda seen to it five years ago."

"Well, ah'll tell you, son—they'll move their asses now."

"Damn tootin'."

"Got damn crooks gonna have a big accountin' for funds all way to Tallahassee."

"Damn right."

"Nuther Jack, ma'am?"

"Thanks, I'm fine."

"Hey, come on over an join us." She was fat, jolly, sort of whorey-looking with her front bicuspid missing, and Jimmy introduced her as Lucille, whose husband had the gas station. "Now you look like you gotta story, don't she look like she got one, huh?" Lucille says.

"She's a writer, Cille. Course she gotta story."

"I knowed it. I knowed she was a writer."

"How'd yuh know?"

"Cause she looks like Jane Fonda, and she's a writer kinda."

"She's a movie star."

"Naw. She's more a women's libber writer . . . whadyah say, uh Faye? She more a women's libber writer or a. . . ."

"Oh heavens, I don't know."

"See, whad I tell yuh, she's both."

Goldchains stuck to his Seven & Seven during this exchange, shaking his head to show he thought it all good fun. After that, Cille settled down to another Miller.

"It's a terrible thing, what's happening." She suddenly brings her head up, the jolly in her gone. She looks defeated. "Hell, we lost half the citrus last year from frost, now we're losing it to flood—ain't nuthin' to do for us poor bastards but go on welfare."

"Oh now, Cille—we don't know it's that bad."

"Hell it ain't, Jimmy. You know well as me. You ever write about things like this, hon?"

The smell of grilled meat sweetened the air, and the buzz and drying and thawing of the Jack made Faye feel pretty good despite the accident and flood and this latest boyfriend sending her back his key.

"Well, not specifically a flood, but I have—only when I've been there though."

"Well, you're there, honeychile. This is it. You lose a crop, you lose your shirt. . . ."

"Cille, that ain't exciting stuff to write about."

"Oh no, that's not true. It is exciting." In a way Faye guessed it was.

"That's okay. You said your name was Faye? I gotta girl named Fayette. Well, bet you never thought you'd wind up spending the night in Ponce De Leon, huh Faye?"

"You're right there, Lucille."

Faye had sat with them at the bar, and there were some others from the bus as well as her—a guy about fifty with a peg-leg, only it wasn't a peg—more like a hoof with part of a moccasin put on the flesh-colored end. He'd made the prosthesis himself after nobody could fit him right, and he said he'd kinda been handy all his life and it seemed natural. But he didn't say it boastfully. He had a kind of ironic good will, and everybody liked him. Especially Faye who was attracted to him in an odd way—he was real to her like he had nothing to prove—his smile bore that out—and she liked his eyes, big llama eyes. When she asked him what he did, he said he manufactured pre-fab houses and bought her a round.

"You gotta lot a guts, mister." Fat Cille showed the gap between her teeth. Hearing the Hoof tell of how he lost his foot cheered her up from her own misery. There were three Mexican migrant workers too, but they sat at the tables and stuck to themselves. And one kid about twenty, dirty blond with an army duffel bag. His nose ran and she thought by the way his face twitched up, he was coming off something.

"Y'all eat hearty, folks." Cheryl, her son Cole, and her daughter-in-law Elise came out with three platters, and pushed some tables together except the Mexicans, who they let be, and served separately.

It was all homestyle. Butter beans, collards, corn, stewed tomatoes, marshmallow salad, and fried okra served in those heavy white vegetable dishes and passed around with plenty of mashed potatoes. Most ordered t-bones except Hoof and Runny Nose, who got the meatloaf. Faye thought it was the best country meal she ever had, and didn't do anything but nod to the conversation. Everyone drank Miller on tap.

"Lord, that hits the spot, don't it." Goldchains sat on her right. He'd been talking about buying land outside Eustis, where Faye was headed with all the rest except Hoof, who said he was going to Mt. Dora.

"Delicious."

"Nice place here, real old-fashioned. There aren't many places like this anymore."

"No."

"Offer still holds. I'd like to buy you that t-bone."

"No really. Thanks."

"Suit yourself. You married?"

"Yes."

"You don't wear a ring."

"No. My husband and I don't wear rings."

"Ah. One of those modern marriages."

"No. We had rings. We both lost them."

"Uh huh. What your husband do?"

"He's a writer too."

"Would I know him?"

"I don't think so."

Hoof looked from her to Goldchains and smiled. She smiled back. He put his finger to his lips, then ear. She put her finger to her nose and nodded.

"C'mon, you ain't married. It's okay. It don't make no difference."

"Sure I am."

"No, you're not. Saw it on the registration."

"Hey."

"Sorry. Used to be in the business. I always notice stuff like that—woman traveling alone—real classy even with the blue jeans—not one you'd see on a bus usually."

"You're kidding. You're a private detective."

"Was. Got my own security business now."

"That's quite a field."

"You better believe it. This past year we quadrupled surveillance systems, dogs and TV monitors."

"You sell all that stuff?"

"Sure do. You never seen so much paranoia. Everybody sees Cubans round every corner."

Faye figured he sold a lot to the dope trade. . . . It'd make sense, just like his gold chains, and the open shirt, and the pompadourish hair made sense.

Cheryl had cleaned off the tables while Cole and Elise traded dirty plates for cherry cobbler à la mode. The Mexicans turned it down, and ordered another round of tequila. They smoked little black cigarillos and played five-card stud.

"It don't look good out there, Faye, it surely don't." Cheryl sat down and massaged her ankles. "Hell, I haven't seen this much goin' on this late since Hurricane Camille. How was it, hon?"

"Real good. I mean it."

"I'm sick of these men. Want to have a little nightcap in your room? I'll fix it with Jimmy."

"Sounds good to me."

Upstairs they exchanged lives as easy as if they'd known each other since high school.

". . . Hell, in my day they'd damn near take you to Okefenokee and shoot you for it, but we wanted to get married anyway—and it's a marvel, this day and age, me only having one man in my life."

"You miss it? Not having more?"

"Did like crazy in my twenties. Used to daydream a lot. What's it like?"

"You get dizzy by it. Eventually you get broken by it."

"You ever wanna get married again?"

"I say I don't but sometimes I do. If you meet someone special, it's the first thing that comes to mind. Even now, the dreams don't change."

"I reckon they don't. We don't change inside. You know, I'll level with you. Lately, I got a bad itch for it. Terrible. Can't pray it away or nuthin, not that there's much chance. I just have that feeling I missed something and it gets me to lying awake nights. Jimmy, he just thinks it's the change yuh know."

All the time Cheryl was saying these things, she'd been smoothing out Faye's clothes, stroking the silk dress before she hung it, laying out the damp undies and jeans before the space heater. Faye knew enough not to try and stop her, or to thank her too profusely.

"You get this in New York?" She held up the purple silk. "Hmm hmm. I don't remember a purple that pretty. Real silk?"

"Yes."

The dress was six years old and only worn to weddings of conservative distant relatives. She hated it.

"Bet it cost."

"A hundred and fifty, six years ago. It's never fit right though."

"Six years ago? Be three, four hundred now."

"I would think. Listen, take it. You'd be doing me a favor."

"Oh no, hon, I couldn't."

"Sure you could. You've been very kind and. . . ."

"I couldn't. Not without paying. . . ."

"Okay. We could work out an exchange. How about tonight's dinner for the dress."

"Hey. But that's not enough."

"Yes, it is. That was the best meal I've had in a while."

"I don't know."

"Try it on at least, see if it fits."

Faye unzipped the back of Cheryl's dress. It was one of those polyester day shifts with flashes of hot pink—easy care through the washer/dryer. Cheryl let it stay in a heap, then treated the mussed silk like gold.

"Smashing."

"It do fit right."

"Have a look. It's definitely you, Cheryl, really."

She was well proportioned—a little thick at the hips but the dress allowed for it. It was one of those styles that could be worn on a thirty-pound weight slide.

"Could you wear it out somewhere to dinner? It's not right for church."

"Oh yes. I'd get some wear out of it."

"Well, there you go. Deal?"

"Deal—well, I do believe I'm a little tipsy."

"Me too."

"Well, I'll just leave you to a good night's sleep and dontchu worry, I'll getcha up in plenty of time. Whatcha like for breakfast?"

"Oh, anything."

"Wanna real Southern one? Biscuits, red-eye gravy, country ham?"

"Are you kidding? That'd be fabulous."

"Well, you jus' sleep tight. I'm gonna tuck in for an hour myself. I wanna pray for the people on the bus. You ever pray? Guess you don't."

"Oh yes. I do."

"You do? You pray?"

"Yes."

"Huh. Well, I didn't mean that you woun't. I declare. I don't know what I mean."

"Oh, I do pray sometimes."

"Well, we could pray for the people on the bus and the flood together."

"Yes, we could do that."

"We could kneel against the bed here, that be all right?"

"Yes."

"We don't have to say nothing."

"No. I'm pretty quiet about it. I do it on the run sometimes."

"I used to do it when the picking season was on—used to pray over the oranges, but that was a long time ago."

Faye and Cheryl knelt down side by side with their elbows on the bed. Cheryl's elbows were chapped, and she still had on the purple silk dress, which made her look haggard, and showed the chicken flesh of her neck. Faye closed her eyes and tried to pray for the bus people, but found herself praying for Cheryl's keeping the lid on until she was through with the change instead. The rain had started again. The overhead light blinked.

After about five minutes, Cheryl said A-MEN, and gave her a pat, took the polyester off the floor still wearing the purple and closed the door as quietly as she could behind her.

Faye put on her ex-husband's t-shirt she wore as a nightgown. She wrote in her journal the events of that evening— quick and sloppy to get it all down. There was a knock on the door, soft enough so as not to wake her if she'd been asleep. She figured it was Cheryl.

"Hi. Look if I'm bothering you. . . ."

"No, not really."

"This is hundred-year-old cognac. Since it's a strange night. . . ."

"Ships passing in the night?"

"Well, we seemed to click."

"Think we'll ever get out of here?"

"Oh sure. Jimmy said the bus'd be in tomorrow. Sheriff phoned in about midnight."

"Well, come in with your cognac then."

He smiled like the whole world loved him. The rain stopped again, but the lights kept flickering.

"You better light those candles. Power's gonna go out. Always does around here."

She lit the candles beside the bed, and on the dresser.

"Can you get it? I've a camping knife with a corkscrew."

"No, I got it."

They sat down side by side on the spread and sipped the cognac.

"Something, huh."

"Yes."

"How come me, Faye?"

"You seemed decent."

"You did too. Isn't much of that around."

"No, not much. Some, though. Do you need help?"

"No, I can do it on my own."

She took off her ex-husband's t-shirt and kissed him.

"Is it cumbersome?"

"No. Easy. See this pin? You just slide it up and off, and it comes open like a door."

"You know what? I think you're a genius."

"No. I just figured if you want anything done right, you better do it yourself."

Faye picked up the half a leg. She felt the heaviness of it, put it close to the candle and looked at the color, which was close to natural flesh. They were still sitting side by side on the spread, his pant leg rolled up, the leg whittled down to skin over bone with a round nub at the end. He looked down at it, and then at her to see what her reaction would be.

"That's a beautiful leg," she said. "God couldn't have made it better."

Motorcycle Man in a Cajun Campground

He had come in on a motorcycle sometime after midnight and they'd given him the slot next to hers. It had stopped raining, though the ground was soaked and half the slots were under a foot of water—so most the campers, those that weren't in vans or RV's were still up and talking.

He was young, nice-looking in an intelligent way but not meant to be intellectual. And although the windshield of the big Harley was full of bugs, and his leather jacket smelled of damp and was cracked, and the fake fur collar tacky with sweat and rain, and his face streaked with road soot—he had the look of a clean person by nature.

The first thing he did was introduce himself to her, but not in an aggressive way. He just went over, said his name was Ned, and offered to help her with the tent, which she'd been retying after an earlier wind had loosened the spokes.

"Been like this long?"

"Just since this morning. Yesterday was beautiful."

"Never been in the South before."

"Oh?"

"Yah. Drove straight down from Michigan."

"You're kidding. How far is it to Louisiana?"

"To where?"

"Lafayette."

"Thousand miles."

"That far and you did it straight?"

"Well, stopped for gas and stuff."

"How long it take you?"

"Twenty hours."

"Twenty! Don't your legs feel funny?"

"Yah. I'm still vibrating, like when you get off a sailboat."

"You sail?"

"Used to. On Lake Michigan. Why, you?"

"Yah, but not much."

"You alone?"

"Uh huh, why? What's funny?"

"Nothing. I mean I wasn't laughing at you. It's just unusual."

"What?"

"A girl camping alone, especially with that little pup tent. It's refreshing."

"Oh yah? Refreshing? I've been soaked ever since I started."

"Started from where?"

"Florida, well the Keys actually—although I guess you might say I live most of the year in New York."

"The Keys? Really? The Keys huh."

"Yah. I decided to camp cross-country for a couple of months."

"I'm impressed."

"Don't be. It isn't that big a deal anymore. Think of it as being professionally homeless for a while."

"But why'd you do it?"

"I wanted to see America."

"But camping alone?"

"It's the best way. You see everything."

"It isn't dangerous?"

"Most the time I stay in campgrounds. It's okay."

"Nothing happened?"

"Once on a beach in the Panhandle. But that turned okay."

"You were attacked."

"No. I was almost attacked."

"What you do?"

"Slept in the car."

"That your car? The silver 'Beemer'?"

"Uh huh. 530i, vintage 1978, damn good year."

"Nice. Very nice."

"Very fast."

"They're great cars."

"It's the love of my life."

"I can see you're proud of it."

"Damn right."

"What happens if you break down?"

"You mean. . . ?"

"Yah, in the middle of nowhere."

"I get out and fix it if I can."

"And if you can't?"

"I pray. It's always worked out. Look, it's started raining again."

They made a run for the bike just as the wind picked up and the first big drops were hitting. She helped him get the bungey cords off and gathered his gear under the tarp while he put up his tent in the slot next to hers.

"I like the way they've got a tarp over these slots, and they're on platforms."

"Yes. Makes a big difference. I hear this area has a lot of cottonmouths."

"Hmm. I'm not much on snakes. You don't see anything more than a garter snake in Michigan."

"Hmm. Are you here for long?"

"Couple of days. I've got a job waiting on the coast."

"Oil?"

"Yah, I'm a drilling supervisor."

"Really. Sounds interesting."

"It's okay. This'll be my first job offshore. What do you do?"

"Write."

"Write what?"

"Poetry, stories, whatever."

"I had a feeling you were something like that."

"Why? Do I look weird?"

"No. You look smart."

"I'm not terribly smart. You don't have to be for writing, just keen."

"Well educated then."

"No, not even that. Especially not that. Are you well educated?"

"I'm over-educated. I have a Masters."

"In what?"

"Civil engineering."

"But that doesn't have anything to do with oil does it?"

"It's not incompatible. Just unnecessary. I was thinking of going into city planning."

"Uh huh. . . ."

". . . But I didn't know what I wanted, not really, and I saw this *National Geographic* about the Gulf Coast and I kept changing majors and jobs, and I'm not married so. . . ."

". . . So you got into oil."

"Right."

"I'll bet your family didn't approve."

"No. How'd you know?"

"It's just the way you are."

"What."

"Oh, I have a feeling about it. Your dad's well off and you didn't do well in school and you probably worked as a carpenter for a while."

"I did. You're uncanny."

"No. Observant. You're hands are rough, but your habits are patrician, and you have what I think of as an upper-middle-class Midwestern accent. Did you know upper-middle-class Midwestern is the standard from which American English is spoken correctly?"

"Whaa. . . ."

"Yah, disc jockeys and announcers speak it, and American lexicographers look to. . . ."

"Oh yah, so then what's your accent?"

"I've lived a lot of places."

"Midwest?"

"Milwaukee, and the East, and the Florida Keys."

"Sounds good."

"Yah, it's good. But it was lonely."

"Yah, I guess it was."

They sat like that, on the mat in front of her pup tent, for hours. She didn't want to turn in and neither did he. So they talked and watched the sky. The clouds were moving faster now, with a sliver of a moon between and it was quite beautiful in a mysterious way—the lightning over the bayous, the eggplant color of the night, listening to the sounds of the campground and the crickets. She told him about Milwaukee—the cottage on Forest Lake outside Madison—being a kid with her own rowboat rigged with a sail. He talked about sailing on Lake Michigan, and they figured out they'd lived on a straight line across the Lake from each other at the same time, although he was nine years younger.

"Why'd you really come down here?"

"You mean—to work?"

"Yah."

"To get away."

"From what?"

"My father. I mean, his business. . . . I mean him. You married?"

"Was."

"I was married too."

"Kids?"

"No. You have kids?"

"No. Ever think of marrying again?"

"Not yet. But I probably will. I did it twice. It's the way I am."

"You've been married twice?"

"Uh huh."

"Bad men?"

"No. Bad marriages. Nice men, actually."

"Hmm. Can't say that myself."

"You can't?"

"No, I never really loved her."

"No one's ever clear on that, Ned."

"Don't you think some are?"

"We're all so fragile about that stuff."

"Yah, maybe we are. But I still never did."

"Then why'd you do it?"

"I don't know. She wanted to. I'd gone to school with her."

"Oh. Well. Common experience."

". . . And my father."

"Common experience and your father . . . I don't have to contend with that."

"What?"

"My father. They're both dead. I have no one to set an anchor to me."

"I'm sorry. . . . But you're pretty down to earth."

"Yah, I am in a way. But adventurous."

"Me too. Once I got out. How long are you here for?"

"I'm not sure."

"That's right, you don't have a timetable."

"No. And I want to get out on the bayou, stuff like that—see Cajun country."

"I just gotta see a guy lives in Lafayette, this oil guy. That's all I gotta do."

"Well, you have a job on the Coast."

"But it doesn't start 'til Thursday."

"Oh. So you have almost a week. There's lots to see. You've never been to New Orleans?"

"No. Never been in the South. Remember?"

"Oh. Right. Well, it's a mysterious place, Louisiana."

"I know. I read about it."

". . . in the *National Geographic*. . . ."

"Right again."

". . . That your mother got you a subscription to. . . ."

"Five years ago. You ever read palms?"

"Come on. I told you, it's all probability shit. . . ."

"You're a pretty girl, real pretty, but you talk like a truck driver."

"You mind?"

"No, it's just strange. Do you want to uhhh. . . ?"

"No, I do not."

". . . Didn't think so. It's just that. . . ."

"Doesn't matter. . . ."

"No it does. I never met anyone like you. . . ."

"It's the rain and being on the road. You're ga-ga."

"I am not ga-ga. What're you doing tomorrow?"

"I'm going to get on a swamp boat if I can find one."

"Could I come?"

"That would be fun, but you better try and sleep, I can tell you need to. . . ."

". . . If you had a baby, you wouldn't be lonely."

"Oh you are ga-ga—you really better get some sleep."

He was still out of it when she got back from the payphone. So she figured she'd do her laundry, since it was two hours 'til the boat went out and she could hear the sounds of the whirring machines and the other campers were over there—the ones she liked talking to. Inside the laundry room, which was nothing more than a screened-in porch with half a dozen washer/dryers, a bunch of the younger ones were standing against the machines cracking jokes.

"Hey hey."

"Hey hey."

"Y'all up early huh. We seen yuh. What's he like?"

"Real nice. Down from Michigan. Did it all in one shot."

"No kidding."

"Where's Carralee-Ann?"

"Feedin' the baby—got damn, it gonna rain again."

"Looks that way."

"Hey, know what! My wife's a painter—you kin write 'bout a painter."

"Sure. What kind of painter?"

"House painter."

"Oh . . . hey, a good one."

"Yup. Only girl housepainter in Francis, Kentucky."

"So now you're gonna take your chances."

"Hey. We gonna get rich on that de-regulated land."

"Not everybody finds oil, do they, Joey?"

"Carralee an me, we're gonna find it, an I can get a job in the meantime."

She remembered most of them by name now . . . the names were too good not to write down . . . especially Carralee-Ann, which she thought particularly pretty, and the ones in the laundry—Burgess, Linda, Joey, and the rest. Their stories were similar, about coming from Oklahoma, West Virginia, Kentucky—because of the free-for-all over de-regs they called it, and a shot at getting in on the oil boom. They were all as white trash poor as something out of the Thirties except their hair was long, they smoked pot, and they looked like something out of Haight-Ashbury 15 years ago, only none of them got beyond high school. Carralee-Ann was 16, with a year-and-a-half-old kid, so she was naturally interested in their hopes for the future, though how any of them could live on peanut butter, cereal, and beer, and look as healthy as they did, was beyond her.

"We was worried 'bout you last night. That guy okay?" Carralee-Ann kicked the screen door closed with her hip. She had Bryan-Joseph in a sling.

"Oh fine."

"He help you with your tent? We seen what. . . ."

"She's okay, Carralee-Ann. He was. Anybody want some ritz crackers?"

"I got a thing of granola bars . . . no please, I'll just get sick if I eat anymore."

"Well, I done picked up the coffee. Hope y'all like it sweet. She put a damn ton a sugar in it."

It was nice what they had in that room. It was the weather that brought them closer, that and her helping with babysitting Bryan Joseph, and them running after her tent when the wind picked up the stakes, and planking the back wheels of her car when she got stuck in the mud. At first it seemed weird she should be driving this fast fancy car and be putting up the smallest tent, but then she explained about the book money and the car, and liking to drive off the main highway— how it was safe. Somehow that sat right with them . . . even though they didn't have a pot and she'd breezed in with this fancy car, they could see it was okay in this case and made an exception.

Once she'd gotten herself situated, she drove the ten miles into Lafayette with the radio playing Cajun music, passing levees which looked to her like something out of Southern Italy . . . and found that out of all the southern states she'd been through in the last month, she could maybe see herself here—with the old houses in Lafayette and the swampiness of the land which had both a primitive and tranquil attitude about it, although she didn't delude herself. It'd be hard to move here if she ever did—unless she got a job at the local college, which was unlikely. Although she didn't rule it out.

"Hey, you're up. Sleep well?"

"Yah, what time is it?"

"Close to nine. I'm surprised you slept through everyone talking."

"Me too. What about the swamp boat?"

"It's outa Breaux Bridge."

"Can I still come?"

"Yah, but I'm leaving in ten minutes."

"We could take the bike."

"What if it rains?"

"We get wet. You don't mind that."

"No. And I like bike rides. Okay."

It was okay, though she started out a little nervous. But then he kept to a moderate speed and seemed as shy with her as she was shaky about him, which ultimately made her relax. And then it was great. The still damp air against them, the cypress and live oaks whizzing by, being pressed against his jacket—the smell of it. They took one wrong turn just short of the levee and wound up in a field of blue cornflowers with no one around—then backtracked and opened it up full, and by the time they finally found the right cut, the Cajun already had his engine running.

The boat was similar to the open, flat-bottomed ones used in the Everglades except it had raised pontoons underneath and a full canopy overhead—fringed like a surrey, and no seats—just benches at the sides. So they sat close, with the captain in front of them. But there were only the three others going: Cotton LeBeau, his wife Pixie, and their granddaughter Angelique, who'd just gotten her divorce final last week and was "getting over it" she said, and the reason they were doing this was, "believe it or not," she said, because it was Granddaddy's seventieth birthday, and he'd never gone "believe it or not" on a swamp boat.

Cotton was a big, jocular guy with the thickest white hair Faye'd ever seen, and a wife as tiny and wizened as he was red-cheeked and expansive. He never bothered to hide anything, he said, and told as how he'd grown up in these parts and made a fortune in oil. And since this was his birthday, he could say what he wanted—and what he thought was that life had been good to him and Pixie—he was proud of being Cajun and then talked Cajun to the captain, who had half a set of teeth, greasy hair, and looked like he'd kill his mother if she crossed him.

At first Ned had been shy. Mostly they were talking to her and occasionally the captain would point to the smoke top of a still and always say, "mon oncle" or "mon cousin" until everyone joined in with "mon oncle." Then Cotton saw the harmonica in Ned's pocket, and coaxed him into playing "When the Saints Go Marching In," with the captain and Cotton singing it in the flat, nasal Cajun she thought was hilarious.

They'd taken what looked to be the main waterway for a while til they lost sight of the levee, then branched off into one of the estuaries, which narrowed down until the canopy would get caught and tangled under long drapes of hanging moss, and you could see the roots of the trees shining iridescent under the water.

It was crazy and special—Ned putting his hand over hers to say as much. The rain starting didn't make any difference. Cotton with his stories of rags to riches, bleached blond Angelique with her portable bar and her offerings of martinis at ten in the morning—in the middle of nowhere—groping up all these estuaries getting soaked by the breeze, and even Pixie, who looked like she'd mind anything adventurous, showing herself to be as hale as her husband . . . the lightning moving in now—dead dark, then like somebody turned a film stobe on . . . eerie . . . Ned with his arm around her, pulling her away from the metal pole, the rain coming in thin sweeps that made the river look like a paint brush was pushing it around . . . the captain laughing with his pint of Four Roses and his "Eet's okay, mes ameeeezzz," flooring the swampboat back to the levee in a zig-zag, and everybody laughing like they weren't going to get struck by lightning and die. By the time they got back in, it was pushing two, and nobody wanted to end it—Cotton saying, "well, hay'ell, we go over Bon Chance and you get best Cajun food there is—be Sunday feast yoh." So that's where they went.

The Bon Chance stood off to one side of a four-Stop-sign crossroads. A square one-story pre-fab in an immense parking lot half-filled with pick-up trucks. Inside, it was jammed—a Cajun band playing "La Vie Triste," which despite the title was an upbeat tune—a dozen or so cloggers dancing—making the floor around them shake. They sat at a logger-style table, drank beer out of pitchers, ate jumbalaya and langoustines. "These are the smallest lobsters I've ever seen," Ned said to Cotton and thereafter Cotton calling him Crawdaddy and laughing to everybody who came up to wish him a "Bon annniiivaaaarsaire," "hey, this boy he be from Meetchigan, he say we got small lobsters here," while Pierre the captain got up and sang one solo with the band, which was how they did it—when the spirit moved—others doing the same thing . . . and she thought with their dark hair and brows, the small, compact stature, they all looked related.

. . . And although Angelique couldn't hold her liquor and cried her way through the shoofly pie about her divorce and her husband going off with someone she thought was her friend, there were enough single guys asking her to dance who knew what the score was—that she'd be a rich woman someday—to make her feel pretty and desired, although for what she needed, it was sad she'd never look the way she wanted to look.

By the time they'd said their goodbyes, it was clear and dark, with the moon coming up. It was enough. Too good. She'd leave in the morning but not tell him til then.

"Don't go."
"I better."
"Why? You don't know what you're doing any more than me."
"I want to stay."
"I want you to stay."
"Why, Ned?"
"You know why."
"Will you think about me?"
"Yes."
"I'll think about you."
"Then, why can't you?"
"Because it's a quest. I have to do it all."

"What's all?"

"The country. America. The West. Death Valley."

"You're gonna camp in Death Valley? Don't."

"I have to."

"But maybe we're in love."

"Maybe. But it's the mystery."

"Will you take my phone number? Where I can be reached?"

"Yes, I'll do that."

"Will you call me, call me if you get into trouble or anything?"

"No, probably not."

"I didn't think so, but I want you to have it anyway."

"This way it's perfect and we're perfect and there'll never be any regrets."

"I checked your tires and the engine while you were paying your bill."

"Thank you. I'm going to think about you a lot. Do you like it here?"

"Yes. It's scary, but I do."

"I do too. Are you nervous about starting work?"

"A little."

"You'll do fine. It's a new life."

"Maybe I'll see you."

"Maybe you will. I'll think about you when I make camp in Death Valley."

"Promise?"

"Promise."

Which was true. She thought about him in New Mexico and up in Utah, though not in Texas because it was too close, and there was a flood which took up her mind, but when she got between Beatty, Nevada, and Lone Pine, California, in the middle she figured of Death Valley and not a soul, and she was frightened. That night in that dry ocean of nothing with a full head of stars, she sat out on the tarp before her pup tent and thought about him and what he was doing, and it made the fear go away.

Thinking West

"Hi honey, what's your story?" was the way it all started, the gal saying it and her saying her name was Moira and she owned the saloon, although she really said "this joint" and it was hard for Faye to believe she actually turned the chair around and sat on it *Blue Angel* style, without so much as a "may I join you." But this was the desert and a whole different ballgame.

"So where you from?"

"Florida Keys. Well, New York and the Keys actually."

"And no man with you! Whoooooeeee, honey, you're a girl after my own heart. Hey Alice! . . . this my daughter, Alice . . . Alice meet Faye, she drove out here all by her lonesome."

"Hey wow!"

"You ain't stayin' at my motel, I woulda remembered."

"No. The Park, camping."

"No kidding, an I thought I was the only one did stuff like that . . . you hunt?"

"Nuh uh."

"Well I hope you gotta gun."

"Nuh uh."

"Even Alice got a rifle, taught her myself. You need one for snakes out here. S'cuse me a minute, that's my boyfriend come in."

Her boyfriend was half her size, a skinny runt of a trucker—

the kind who sits facing out from the bar stool. Moira put
a beefy arm around his neck, and Faye heard her call out
for a well-done steak.

Actually it had started before—Faye's feeling that she'd
crossed the line into the West—it started when she turned
off 10 onto the road that parallels the Texas state line, a
two-laner with her first view of the table top mesas which
bordered southern New Mexico. What happened was strange.
One minute the sky was so open and blue and the air fragrant,
dry, the smell of the desert, the clouds outlined . . . and
the next it started raining, which was the last thing she'd
have expected for this part of the country in July. So then
she's pushing eighty, with the tape recorder going, and she's
catching herself up talking about where she's been that day,
what she ate, about the people and Mexican influence in San
Antonio, about the Hotel Mengis where Teddy Roosevelt
stayed and that it seemed to retain its authentic flavor as
opposed to the new fancy hotels down beside the water,
and the Alamo next to the Mengis, that didn't mean much
to her, and that she was ashamed to say, what made the
most impression on her was the fried sweet bread you could
get at these little stops in the middle of nowhere that was
called sopapilla or something like that and reminded her of
the fresh, raised doughnuts of her Midwestern childhood and
what you can't find in New York. And next to that, the
floods of the area around Corpus Christi where she was
forced to turn inland instead of continue down to Brownsville
which had been her intention. And it had been the first time
she'd seen water up to the second step of houses, and police
guiding motorists to detour roads. But then afterwards the
sun came on strong and she drove through that flat brown,
dusty landscape which bordered between agriculture and the
scrub bush beginnings transitional to desert. Texas was a
dusty state. She saw it on her windshield and on the faces
of the people in small towns. She had heard Dallas and
Houston were like the oasis of culture that Eastern cities

used to be, and the inhabitants went at elegance with a vengeance. But she had no use for cities and avoided them, except for San Antonio, which still had the feel of the old Texas. But Texas had not "felt" West to her. Nor did it feel "South." It had its own set of cultural, geographical statements to make, and she could not pigeonhole them.

But when she took the turn-off, and saw the mesas and smelled the desert, and the biggest hornet she'd ever seen flew in her window while she was pushing eighty, and her with her fear of hornets—slowly, unthinkingly rolling up the newspaper with one hand and holding it out to where the hornet rested on the dash, and the hornet getting on and she passing it in front of her nose, neither braking nor accelerating—and with one hand at ten o'clock on the steering wheel, passing the hornet inches before her eyes and carefully . . . very carefully . . . with a firm hand, slipping the newspaper through the third-open window until the hornet was out and the speed of the car and the wind dislodged it and then realizing what she'd done, was incredibly proud of herself.

That's when she felt she was West. She felt a foreignness and openness and leanness of thinking, erased of useless detail . . . she felt she was "thinking" West. And then it'd started to rain and she crossed the state line into New Mexico.

As soon as she crossed the line she was in desert. Real desert. The kind with tall cactus and sand. Only it was raining. The first night she stopped in White City and took in the Carlsbad Cavern and the bats and that was okay except all the tourists being there neutralized the wonder she was meant to experience and she took off at daybreak and resented the souvenir shops and expensive dinner she'd had the night before, and kept driving straight West like she had no control over it, only this wonder at being in desert, and feeling and thinking West. Which was hard because the roads were circuitous, and were becoming hilly and at one point her car lost power climbing, and she had to stop in Ruidoso and lucked out on the third try with a mechanic who told her, under the circumstances, he was going to show her what her car was all about—and it had started raining again, but they went at it under the hood, and he disconnected the pollution devices and readjusted the engine because he said it was vapor lock from driving at altitudes of 8,000 feet and better, and then after four hours of that, only charged her sixteen dollars. And she thought this guy with his run-down cowboy boots and his black GI pal were the last true gentlemen of the earth.

That night she stayed outside Ruidoso because the rain was coming too hard to see well at night and her eyes were tired from the desert. The next day was clear and beautiful, and she saw the first large grouping of Indians outside Tulerosa where she stopped and ate a Mexican breakfast of sopapilla and re-fried beans. The Indian women had on colorful skirts and both men and women wore silver belts and necklaces. She thought, by the look of them, they were rich and proud. In Almagordo, some less prosperous Indians were selling silver in the market, and she bought several rings and a bracelet. The woman who sold them to her was young, with an open moonface and a gentle manner. The bracelet was made by her husband she said, but she had designed and signed the rings. The price was fair and Faye didn't barter.

Then she drove to White Sands and though the temperature was over a hundred she wasn't hot. At half-hour intervals rattlesnake advisories came on over the radio, and when she thought she might be taking a long walk in the desert she turned off at an outfitters and bought a snakebite kit and found herself a long stick. The snakebite kit turned out to be nothing more than one of those chemical ice packs that would be used as a tourniquet, which was next to useless so she kept it in the car, taking only her knife, a razor blade, her walking stick, and a camera in its bag with extra film, and walked a mile out into White Sands, which is hard to do. There was nothing but white powder, dunes of it . . . hillocks of sink-in-white nothing. She thought snowshoes might have worked on it. The walk back and forth—with times to pause—took four hours. She saw a few rattlesnakes, but they kept out of her path. The conservation officer at the entrance had said after rain in the desert, they come out to dry themselves in the sun. In the valley beyond one of the dunes she saw three curled up together. She took half a dozen photos with a zoom, more to show them bunched up that way than for the danger of it. She experienced no fear, but moved cautiously, taking many rolls of film just of the sky, which without other frame of reference dominated everything—the color of the sand and her sense of distance and the movement of day into evening—until upon her return to the first dune, where by then others had gathered, she watched the sun set. Although it was not a sunset the way it was in tropical places which appears volcanic with red and gold. It had more to do with the values of blue and the slide into violet and black—and before that a kind of apricot on the sand. But it wasn't the color that got her, or the snakes and the fact she wasn't afraid of them, it had more to do with understanding the way it is with the West, and how it affected her thinking, which had become simple—a series of needs and impressions as unshaded as a forest without foliage, and where it seemed to go on forever and there was nowhere to hide and there was no desire to hide.

. . . So by the time she'd found the campground outside Rincon, it was closing in on ten, and after pitching her tent and unrolling the bag and slab of foam she used underneath— which took less than twenty minutes—she went over to Moira's Motel and Saloon, which said in neon, "We Never Close Our Kitchen."

It was a touristy-looking place, done in Mexican style with the stucco arches and wagon-wheel chandelier and Indian blankets on the wall. The bar had a placard next to it saying it had been made in 1872, and that Jesse James got drunk before it. There were fake Remingtons in plastic-made-to-look-like-wood frames, but the people there looked local and the license plates outside were mostly New Mexico. And it was big. Big enough to have a cathedral ceiling to suspend the wagon wheels from and outsized round tables that looked the kind where cowboys gambled, according to the movies. There weren't more than about twenty of these tables and Alice showed her to one of them, and put down the menu, which was laminated on a chopping board. She was a big girl, close to six feet, slim but strapping, and with thick blond hair to her waist. She wore a white cowgirl outfit with leather fringe and silver buttons, the skirt came just below a pair of sturdy thighs, and she was clear-complected, perky, and aggressively friendly.

Faye knew everyone glanced over, but she was used to that—being alone—and looked at the menu, which only included meat, chicken, and eggs—ordered huevos rancheros and a beer, and a breakfast steak because she was so hungry after the desert, and then wrote in her diary to avoid the stares until they went away.

That was when Moira came over . . . after checking her out from the bar, though Faye had already spotted her by sneaking glances while she was writing, which was her way of avoiding anything nasty but seeing what was going on. And already she'd figured Alice was Moira's daughter by the blond hair, and the size of their similar noses.

"Listen you gonna be around for awhile?"
"Well, I uh. . . ."
"Stick around. I'll take you out to my ranch tomorrow. We could do some riding."
"You have a ranch?"
"Small one. Jus' two hundred acres, got horses though. What do you say?"
"Sounds fantastic."

"You can ride can't you . . . I don't give lessons or nothing."

"Sure I can ride. I mean I'm not Annie Oakley but I can ride."

"Well, then. Come over here around eleven and we'll go out."

"Where is it?"

"Westfork, ten miles give or take. Can you shoot? I know you said you don't have a gun."

"No."

"Well I'll learn yuh, we need to git rid of rattlers. Jack, my man over there, got bit again yesterday."

"And he's not in the hospital?"

"Naw. It was an old one. Didn't put out no venom. They don't always. Third a all your bites they don't. Didn't know that, didyah city slicker?"

"No I sure didn't."

"You shoulda seen him the first time though. God, six footer got him. I didn't think he'd pull through an you know what, this'un got him the exact same place . . . on the knee in the same trench and both times on horseback. Anyhow you willin' to do that?"

"God, Moira, I don't know. Can I think about it and let you know tomorrow?"

"Shore. You can come even if you don't."

"Has there been a problem recently?"

"Yup. Just this year. Damndest thing. It's the rain done it. Hundred cases of snakebite just in the last month. That's more than last year put together. I've never seen so many, and they're coming close in, which they never did before. Killed two of my horses."

"I'll let you know tomorrow."

She told herself she wouldn't get into her tent before she made up her mind. But she was having a hard time staying awake, and with even the Park Ranger cautioning her so she had to keep her flashlight on though there wasn't a stir and the beam took away from seeing the stars . . . finally she zipped the front flap, and went fast asleep before she resolved it.

She woke up from the nightmare, and it was pitch and the luminescent dials on the travel alarm said 4:30. It was cold but the hair at the base of her neck was soaked and she knew it was useless to try for more sleep and switched on the flashlight. It'd been about Africa, about her mother and her driving the black Packard through a desert village. She was about three or four, the car was a convertible, and there was a great deal of dust rising up from the tires, and on either side of the road were round huts with high, thatched roofs coming to a point. They were driving fast and she had turned around beside her mother to see the dust kick back in the road, and saw her father running after the Packard . . . running and pleading with her mother to stop, and behind him was a huge cobra with his hood the width of the car risen up and sailing on its tail in pursuit of her father.

She begged her mother to stop but she wouldn't, and the snake was gaining, and the last image before waking was of her father running, fists clenched and arms bent like a man in a race, with his big, round face full of tears.

She wasn't much on the meaning of dreams, but since it was the most vividly terrifying dream she could remember having as a grown-up, she tried to think in terms of what it said to the unresolved question of whether she'd go out and shoot rattlesnakes with Moira. It seemed obvious at first the dream meant she should do it, but then she considered the mother in the dream and found her indistinguishable in her image from Moira, although the saloon keeper was big and brassy and her mother had been conservative, although not without a certain risqué sense of humor now and again, like the time she put the flashing Christmas lights in her brassiere for a New Year's party.

By seven, she was still in her tent undecided. And it wasn't that she'd hesitate killing an animal that threatened her. But

she hadn't been threatened. Not out in White Sands when
she saw them massed in the valley, nor even . . . and she
projected it back . . . with the huge hornet she put out of
her car with the newspaper.

She decided the issue only when she walked through the
swinging doors at ten-thirty and waited for Moira, who was
still over at the motel.

"So whatcha decide?"

"I'd like to come. Can I come and have you show me,
and then if I can't shoot that'd still be all right? It's the best
I can do."

"Yah. That'd be all right. Hell, the only reason I asked
yuh was I liked you, not too many women out here—yuh
know, who are hearty . . . be good to chat. Didn't mean
to scare you."

"No, it's not that. It's the killing, frankly."

"You a nun or something?"

"No, a writer."

"Yah, that's what I figured at first, but then. . . ."

"Oh I'm kind of a peacenik."

"You *are*. Shoot. I'm a Republican."

"Really."

"Hell, yes. Headed up the Republican Women's Club in
El Paso when I was married."

"Huh."

"Well, that don't mean I'm a hawk or anything like that.
Besides everybody's gotta decide things for themselves. And
I'm pretty women's lib when it comes to some things, but
I think like a man when it comes to others."

"Uh huh."

"You know what I say, Faye?"

"What?"

". . . It takes all kinds and that's what makes America
great. Cause I wouldn't want it any other way. I mean, would
you? Think about it."

"No. I like the differences."

"Just as I say. That you can be a peacenik as you say and me, a Republican, and we can be friends. Hell, you couldn't do that in Russia."

"No, I guess not. Too much at stake."

"You better believe it. Well, hop in, this my pride and joy, don't see too many regulation jeeps, do you?"

"Not off army bases."

"That's just where I got it. My Dad's a retired colonel."

"Were you an army brat?"

"Yup, sure was."

Moira talked about going to high school in Okinawa, and said a few words in Japanese, and how her husband had been murdered by a Mexican and it'd taken a while before she stopped hating Mexicans, but she did, and with the inheritance money she bought the motel and saloon from her brother, who thought she'd never make a go of it, but she did, though it'd been tough for awhile, and she went without a man for several years, but she had to be careful what with raising Alice and all, and it was a damn good thing Buster came into her life when he did, because she'd gotten so lonely she thought she was drying up into one of those old-before-their-time widows and he'd made her young again, and she was happier now than ever—and wasn't it funny, she just turned fifty and she felt sexier now than at twenty.

They went off the two-laner onto a dirt road about half a mile. It was all fenced in with a big barn and corral, a stone hacienda-style, single-level house. There were chickens and four goats, and several Mexican workmen. Moira took her on a tour first, which didn't take long. Three bedrooms, a living room/dining room, and not in the best repair. Her bookcases were full of back issues of *Life* and *Reader's Digest*. She was proud of the microwave. After that, she took Faye over to the gun cabinet and explained what each firearm was, selected two mid-sized rifles, and took her behind the barn. The instructions took half an hour. Faye's shoulder hurt, and her ears were ringing.

"Well, now you know. Whether you ever use one or not."

Next, the Mexican foreman led out the horses and between him and the two of them, they saddled up, though Faye had forgotten most of what she'd done every summer as a child. Like everything since she'd been in New Mexico.

It didn't bother her, though. She felt that clarity and lack of fear come again which had been growing since the hornet and the mesas and the desert, and once they cleared a couple of passes around the corral, Faye felt comfortable enough to get up to a canter, with the rifle in its leather holder aside her left leg. Nor had it bothered her shooting the rifle, though she'd always been terrified of guns. And the only thing that swayed her sense of well-being was the not-knowing if she would or wouldn't.

A little ways out, Moira's boyfriend, Buster, joined them. He was on a pinto which she'd never seen before. Black and white, built short and very fast. They were on bays. While Moira and Buster set up the route, Faye watched the vultures and took in the faint yellow sun and the brown mountains shimmering with heat waves a long ways off. Here it was relatively green, with grass and trees along the bank of a small river. Further away the trees grew shorter, less leafy, and you could see yucca and sagebrush and mesquite. Moira's herd of horses were mostly by the river and under trees, but you could see half a dozen running out beyond. It looked like what a ranch should look like.

They trotted out in a line, with the men first and Faye bringing up the rear, and everyone but her with their rifles out and resting in front of the saddlebow. She saw the trench Moira had been talking about . . . more a ditch on the other side of the river and leading out towards the beginning of the mountains . . . the horses weren't too keen on going down and it took Faye three tries, with Moira calling back, "Rusty Ho!" before her horse joined the procession, and they took the ditch at a walk and weren't far in before Buster and the foreman fired, dismounted, and placed two diamondbacks in the bag, and she only saw what they were because Buster held one up in each hand. And that went on for over an hour, walking the trench and the horses occasionally rearing up, although at the end of the procession Faye hadn't seen anything, and her horse—except wanting to turn around now and again—stayed pretty much to the pace.

. . . Until it was after two, when they dismounted to water the horses and eat the sandwiches and beer the foreman brought. And it was a funny thing with this kind of heat— no one sweat that much, but a kind of lethargy set in, not fatigue exactly, but a languorous feeling. The men had bagged seven rattlers between them and Moira two, and Faye's rifle was still in the holder. They'd been sitting at a picnic table under a bank of palms surrounded by sagebrush with a small patch of grass before it gave way to sand. Faye put her head down on her arms and fell asleep for five minutes. When she woke, Moira was laughing at her.

"Does that to you."

"I never fall asleep during the day."

"You would if you lived out here." She'd smiled, and the men went behind the sagebrush, and Faye helped Moira clear away the remains of the food . . . which was when she saw one—a big rattler—not ten feet from where Moira stood bending over the table—and Faye took Moira's rifle that had been propped against the bench, and cocked it, and blew its head off . . . and thought nothing much about it, even after she left Rincon and was coming into Albuquerque, which had the feel of a big city—neither Eastern nor Western. She had no feeling about it at all, except she refused the skin, and told Moira to give it to Alice.

A Real Man

He had a belly on him, but it wasn't a pot belly, and looked solid against the cowboy shirt, and he wasn't as tall as she first thought, and he wasn't young but it was hard to tell with a man like that, and if you took him apart, he wasn't handsome. His skin was sunburned and leathery, and pitted especially around the nose, and on the surface of his cheeks you could see a small road map of broken capillaries, but the features fit. It was a good strong straight nose, maybe a little too broad, and the lips were chapped but full, and his teeth were long and even—though there were nicotine stains along the edges, but his eyes were what got her . . . or maybe it was the tan skin that made them more white and almost turquoise and full of the sun when he grinned, and he was the type to grin, not smile, with a full burst of lines around each one, and the minute she walked up to his concession, and he looked at her, they both knew something else was going on.

All she wanted was to rent a mule or a horse and go down into the Canyon, but he said she had to go in a tour, and it was basically a half-day arrangement, and maybe she *was* a little huffy when she told him *she wasn't interested* in a tour, because he came on like Attila.

"Lady, you are jus' full of bull, you know that. You are full of bull." . . . like he was going to take a swipe at her,

like some big bear . . . and then they both started laughing
at themselves, she—because she was tired after the long drive
and the altitude, and all the tourists at the Canyon. And
maybe it was the coming to the Canyon. How she hadn't
expected to suddenly see it off the road as she was driving.
How big and vast . . . and seeing the Painted Desert like
that. So she'd pulled over, and Ellen got out her Nikon with
the six different lenses and started whistling "Diamonds are
a Girl's Best Friend," while Faye felt overwhelmed. So overwhelmed by coming upon the Canyon like that with no
preparation she got mad—mad at Ellen for not being less
of a damn priss and more of a sport—mad at the world for
this kind of beauty—mad at herself for having invited Ellen
to join her in Santa Fe and then assuming she'd want to
camp, which she didn't, and she couldn't read directions
worth a damn, and it had brought out the worst in both of
them. So this Stan Grabel with his drawl and his tours into
the canyon when she wanted to get away from "Diamonds
are a Girl's Best Friend" and the tourists was the last straw.

"I do truly apologize ma'am, honestly. See, I just had 6,000
Japanese wanting to take my picture, and I got it to my gills,
and here's this real pretty, smart-mouthed woman who wants
to get herself kill't and it's ten minutes 'til I close up. Listen,
how 'bout I buy you a beer—can I do that? Can I buy you
a beer, and say I'm sorry, and then we'll talk about fixing
you up with something you'll like, I promise you that, how
about it? I just have to close up."

"No, look. It was my fault. What the hell do I know. Let
me buy you a beer."

"No. I had no right."

"Well, you have to protect yourself."

"We get a lot of wiseacres who don't know nuthin' and
wind up suing you."

"Oh, you have to be careful."

"Lord, I never learn."

"Well. The beer's on me."

"Not with me it ain't."

"Oh all right then."

"What's your name, Slim."

"Faye. Listen, can I meet you in a half-hour? I haven't moved my gear in yet."

"Yup. But not here, I don't drink here."

"I can understand that."

"Know that place right before the Park?"

"I remember passing it."

"Buddy's, it's called. I could pick you up, if you don't mind the truck."

"No, I'll meet you there."

When Faye told her friend Ellen about meeting Stan for a drink and what did she think—Ellen called him a fat old man.

"How the hell can you say that!"

"Well, he *is* a fat old man. Probably not very bright either."

"You are incredible, Ellen. All you like is fags."

"Smart and beautiful fags and rich fags."

"Well, I'm going."

"Go."

"I am."

"Go."

"You want to come?"

"No. I want to do my nails and take a bath and smoke a joint."

"Look. I don't have to go."

"Go. Seriously, go."

"You don't think it's dangerous, do you?"

"Oh Jesus no. He's a fat old man but he's not dangerous. God."

"He isn't fat and he isn't old, Ellen. You think any man's ugly who doesn't look like Rudolf Nureyev."

"Bet he smells like manure."

"So what."

"Bet he sleeps with his horse."

"Bet he's straight."

"He's straight and he sleeps with his horse. Go. Don't get too drunk."

"I won't get too drunk. Don't get too stoned."

"I'm not driving."

They had sorted out the packs and put stuff into the tiny closet, and Ellen was smoking the dregs of a roach, sitting cross-legged on one of the twin beds.

"You shouldn't have come, Ellen, if you didn't want to rough it."

"I'm not a camper, and I didn't expect you to snap at me all the time."

"You've been a putz."

"You can't talk to me that way."

"Well, I just did."

"Look, I'm going through changes."

"Then you shouldn't have come."

"Well, I'll go then."

"Don't go, just stop being a putz."

"Don't say that, Faye. You're the putz. A bossy putz."

Faye put on some lipstick and rouge, and then wiped it off. She figured he liked her the way he saw her, which was haggard and sunburned and without lipstick and rouge and that was the way she'd have a beer with him—besides it wasn't a date. But Ellen was a drag, and what to do about Ellen, who in the city with her elegant gay men, who were actually very nice, and her books out and her smarts, was a wonderful friend and there was much Faye loved about her, but out here the fancy writer stuff looked ridiculous, and she ought to take off the jewelry.

"Listen I'm going. And I'm sorry I called you a putz. It's just that I like him and you called him a fat old man."

"Well he is. But I accept your apology. Where'd you put the wine?"

It was only a few miles up the road, but she caught the light just as the sun was going down, so she stopped for a minute to see the colors on the Painted Desert—and then there was a whole meadow filled with grazing deer—a couple of huge bucks amongst them with mature antlers, and by the time she reached Buddy's Saloon, she was full of awe at what she'd just seen—the size of it, and the Colorado River like some tiny worm a mile down.

"Sorry I'm late."

"You aren't late, Slim. Bet you stopped to see the sun."

"I did. And the deer."

"So tell me. . . ."

He was leaning half on the stool when she came in, and then he stood up for her, and you could tell by the way everyone talked to him, that he was well known and liked. He showed her to a wood booth, and grinned, "What's your story, Slim?"

She always got asked that since she'd been in the West, and she had it down to a minimum of words now.

"I'm a writer. Poetry and stories. Sometimes I get lucky and sell something and make enough money to take off on camping trips like this."

"I pretty much figured you for something like that. Don't much like talking 'bout it do you?"

"Not much. More interesting what you do. What do you do?"

"You mean renting horses and stuff? Let's see. . . ."

He ordered two beers and two shots of whiskey when she said she'd have whatever he was having, she didn't care, and he smelled of soap and maybe a little manure but all and all it was a good smell, and he was smoking Lucky Strikes, and she took one of them from him though she smoked filters, and tried not to laugh when he struck a kitchen match on his boot, and put it out between his fingers after lighting her cigarette.

"Well, would you call yourself a cowboy?"

"Well, I'd say I was strictly speaking more of a horse man than a cowboy and I'm certainly not running that old hairy joke by you. . . ." laughing in spite of himself like she was too urban inbred to get his stupid non-joke.

"So you're a whoresman, that so."

"Naw, I'm harmless enough. So you want to go into the Canyon. You're a pretty sharp girl, Slim. Bet you ride English."

"I ride what's at hand if it isn't too spirited, and if you stop putting me on, I won't laugh at you either—deal?"

"You're some piece of work. Deal. Well, I still can't let you go in without a guide. Those are Park rules, not mine . . . but you can do the trails around here—I can get you on a horse around here, and for much less."

"No, I wanted to go in."

"I don't blame you. It's really something."

"I guess you never go down anymore."

"Sometimes I take long camping trips in, three weeks or better . . . at least I have. I split my time. Got a ranch, too."

"Raise horses?"

"Yup. Stud farm."

"Ah hah. And the Canyon?"

"I own the concession. Got one on the South Rim too."

"How do you get back and forth?"

"Got a plane."

"Oh."

"What do you think I do, jump?" which got him grinning again, and she watched the eyes turn into those sunbursts, and he had such an off-hand way about everything—like he loved his life—it was infectious, and she started grinning back. "I don't expect I've met a girl like you in a while," he said still grinning and she figured he'd been with most of the good-looking women in the bar including the bartender, and that they didn't seem to mind, and liked him more for it, but she had no illusions.

"What do you call a while?"

"A while—WHILE, Slim, you got some mouth on you."

"Back to the horses."

"Back to the horses. Say, you want to see something? You're a writer, you people always want to see things."

"Like what?"

"Wild horses, mustangs."

"Are there any around?"

"Out in the desert there are. Bunch of us are going. You want to come?"

"In the desert with you? I don't know you."

"You know me, Slim, and I know you."

"I don't trust you."

"Sure you do. You just don't trust the fact you trust me."

"You're right, I don't. And I have my girl friend with me."

"Well, bring her. She the one with the jewelry?"

"That's her."

"Well, bring her, we'll make an Annie Oakley out of her."

"She doesn't want to be Annie Oakley. She wants to reach samadhi."

"That so. She workin' her way up the chakras, is she. Didn't think I knew what samadhi is, didyah, Slim."

"I guess not. I'm sorry. I really am an ass."

"A smart-ass."

"A smart-ass, yes. How *do* you know?"

"I was stationed in India."

"In?"

"The Marines."

"You like it?"

"The Marines?"

"India."

"Parts of it. I didn't like people dying in the street. But they do that in New York too."

"Yes."

"And you like it? New York."

"Part of it. But I don't like what you don't like. Besides I'm not a city girl."

"No? Where else you live?"

"The Keys."

"Florida Keys?"

"Uh huh."

"And you ride horses."

"Once in a while. When I was a kid, but that was in the Midwest."

"And you write books."

"Yes. And you come from where . . . let me pay for that."

"No. I come from here."

". . . and you have a ranch and a family."

"A ranch and two ex-wives some distance apart and a hundred head of horses."

She took her money out again, but he put his hand over hers and squeezed, and they locked eyes, but neither one of them thought this was anything more or less than part of the dance. The bartender turned the lights down low, the waitress kept them in pretzels and kept saying "what can I do yuh for, Stan" and Faye could feel she was getting a little tight on the whiskey and beer.

"No. No more. The altitude's getting to me."

He excused himself for the men's, and she watched while a couple of grungy-looking cowboy types clapped him on the back and looked over at her for a minute . . . and saw how he got out of it, since by his expression he was—she thought—treating her with what amounted to respect.

She figured it was pushing seven, because the live music advertised for that time was starting up, and someone had pulled the plug on the juke box. They were local country western and not very good, with the man on the guitar off by a beat, and they dedicated the first tune to Stan Grabel and his mountain lion, and everyone got a kick out of that, so she figured the mountain lion might not be a mountain lion.

"They dedicated a song to you, did you hear?"

"I heard."

"A mountain lion? I don't think so."

"That's my last ex-wife. They called her the mountain lion."

"Really."

"She rode one in a rodeo. Folks want to get us back together, and she's here."

"Oh. Maybe I should go."

"No."

"Well. I don't want to stand in the way of romance."

"You know, Slim, you don't win nuthin' being that way."

"What way?"

"So tough. Like you aren't interested."

"I'm interested."

"So am I and you know it. So shut up. Now, how about those horses."

"In the desert?"

"Yup."

"When?"

"Tomorrow."

"Tomorrow?"

"Yah, unless you want to take the tour into the Canyon."

"No . . . but my girl friend."

"Let her come or not come."

"You don't mess around, do you."

"No and neither do you. Want some dinner?"

"No."

"Neither do I."

"What time tomorrow?"

"Six."

"In the morning!"

"Yup. It'll take two hours to get out there."

"Where should I meet you?"

"I'll pick you up. I know where you are."

"You know everything, don't you?"

"No. I don't know your last name."

Ellen thought she was crazy going out in the desert with

this guy and his cowboys, and she'd rather take the helicopter ride into the Canyon and shoot pictures instead, and what did Faye know about riding anyway. She never saw Faye on a horse. And Faye came back with—that was because all she and Ellen ever did before together was look at art and go shopping and hang out with other writers and her aesthete boyfriends, and she'd never cared about any other side to her. So the women beat that around, and Faye was a little tight and exhausted from all the driving, and Ellen was stoned, which always made her sardonic, and both of them got into their bunk beds resenting the other.

The next morning Faye was up at five. She refilled her canteen, packed a salami, a towel, sunblock, her heavy-duty polaroid dark glasses, toilet water, the snake stick, and a tube of lip balm. She took a shower, washed her hair, put it back in a pony tail, and put on the jeans that fit her the best. Ellen was awake but still in bed.

"Listen Faye, I don't think I want to do this."

"Do what?"

"Stay at the Canyon with you. We were going to do things together."

"I asked you to come along. He said it too. You're just ornery."

"I'm civilized. I do things in a civilized way."

"Whistling 'Diamonds are a Girl's Best Friend' when you get to the rim of the Canyon isn't civilized. It's sacrilegious."

"Oh you're impossible. You think going out with some redneck. . . ."

"He isn't a redneck."

"Well, what is he? He's a fat old man."

"He isn't fat and he isn't old and he's probably more civilized than anyone we know."

"Please. Spare me the Damon Runyon."

"To hell with you Ellen."

"See, that's just what I mean."

"Well I'm going. You can still come."

"I don't think so. I think I'm going to catch the bus to Phoenix."

"Suit yourself."

"I can't understand you, Faye. You're missing an opportunity to do something worthwhile just to hang out with some, oh never mind."

"What opportunity, Ellen?"

"The helicopter. Going into the Canyon."

"I have every intention of going in. What are you talking about? I'm going in by mule, probably tomorrow."

"By mule. When you can see it in a helicopter with views on both sides."

"Yah, just like the pioneers."

"Please. Spare me."

"Spare yourself. What you're saying is if I go to the desert with this guy, you're leaving. If I stay here, would you stay?"

"Yah. I probably would."

"Go to Phoenix, Ellen. Or you can come with us."

"Please. Spare me. I'm going to Phoenix."

He came up and called her "Slim" but low, and he must have heard the tail end of the conversation, because he didn't knock, but just went back to the truck and waited, and when she got out there the sun was just coming over the black pines and it was beautiful.

"Sounds like your girl friend doesn't like your goin'."

"No."

"Why don't I have a word with her."

"You want to?"

"Sure. Calm the waters."

"Okay, but she isn't dressed."

"I can talk through the screen."

Which he did while she watched the dawn and listened to the sounds of mountain night receding with the purple, and she only half made out the exchange, but he came back a couple of minutes later, grinning and shaking his head.

"Well, she's gonna stick with her helicopter but at least

she doesn't think I'm some kind of A-rab or something, so I said maybe she'd like to join us after for barbecue."

"You're a charming sonofagun aren't you."

"Hey, it helps. I'm in the public relations business."

"You could have fooled me."

He helped her into the truck, which was one of those ones with a high cab, and a long trailer which held four horses. He said two other guys were coming, and a married couple, but they weren't going to meet them until the desert started. That was where they'd get on horseback and the others'd take the jeep. Then he pointed to the thermos and told her to pour them some coffee.

The first hour they were both pretty quiet. It was slow going, with the winding road down mountain and hauling the horses, and it was quiet and clear, and she was "thinking West" the way she had when she was in White Sands, with everything simple, and it was lovely. It was just lovely.

She lit a Lucky and put it in his mouth, then lit one of her own, "It's beautiful here."

"I never get tired of it. Tired of some things. But not this."

"I know what you mean."

"How could you know? You never sit still long enough to know what I mean, Slim. Here you're camping around the country and you go down to the Keys and sometimes you're in New York City. Tell me something."

"What?"

"You ever stop?"

"I stop. Sometimes when I'm going I feel I'm stopped."

"Well it's a plain life out here."

"Clear."

"Yup. Clear. People aren't clear. But the land is, unless some spit and polish in Washington wants to change it all around."

"Money rules."

"It don't rule everyone. It rule you?"

"No. I'm very bad about that."

"Well, take a good look today, Slim, because by the time I'm dead and you're a little old lady it's gonna be gone. All damn gone."

"No."

"They'll find a way. They'll blow it up or build those condos or something. Oil, most likely. They'll de-reg the land and put wells in the Canyon."

"No."

"Who's gonna stop it? You? Me?"

"All of us."

"No, no one can stop it."

They kept talking about the land and the government, and the fact there was coming a day where there'd be no place to go, until they both got too philosophical and stopped talking for a while, and just watched the sun spraying the tall pines and then everything heating up so she helped him off with his jacket and took off her own, and they both put on their hats.

"God."

"Yup, God."

"It's fabulous. It's pink."

"Changes color with the time of day."

They had met up with the others at one of those scenic vista lay-bys bordering the desert, and they didn't have much time for talking after that. Jan and Billy—who had the ranch next to Stan's—would take the jeep; and they and the two other men would get on the horses. She liked Jan and Billy a lot right off. She was somewhere in her early forties, friendly, good-natured; and Billy was polite and funny. The two other men, Hank and Lester, worked for Stan on the South Rim concession and they seemed all right as well, but she especially took to Jan and Billy, who were the kind of earthy, common-sense people you trusted right away. And although she was nervous about the riding, which she'd only done a little of on the trip and that in New Mexico on a snake shoot, she managed well enough, which was partly because Stan had given her a horse that was so broken in he was practically sway-backed.

"You weren't taking any chances, were you?"

"He's a good horse."

"If you can get him in third."

"He's a good solid horse."

"Does he understand giddeyup?"

"You wanna ride my Sam?"

"No, I better not."

"Well then, stop your complaining."

Actually she liked that the horse was slow and Stan told the boys to go ahead they'd catch up, so they could go at a walk and he'd been pointing out the eight different kinds of cactus you could see right off and things about geology— what made the desert all those colors—and the geological history of the area. And he didn't do it in a preacherish fashion, he just talked as if he loved it and he loved telling about it.

After a while she got her horse up to a gallop, and they went that way for the half-hour it took to get to where the others were.

"Well, how you like it, Faye?"

"God's country, Jan."

"Amen to that. How 'bout a beer?"

"Sure, can I help you with that."

Jan was laying out the food and beer. Faye took the salami out of her saddle bag, handing it to her, while the men went in single file, unison, one hand at the top of their fly, behind the jeep, and both the women broke out in giggles.

"They're all just big babies. I raised five of them, and they're all two years old when it comes to their pecker or their bladder. And they say women always gotta go. Hell, I'm a camel."

"Me too."

"So Stan told me about you. You're quite a gal."

"Thank you."

"Ever think of moving West?"

"Well, no."

"Healthy place to raise a kid."

"It's a little late for that."

"Oh, you never know."

So then everybody had a beer and sat around eating sandwiches and got into the salami, which they asked about. Faye told them she'd smuggled it back from Yugoslavia, and the closest thing to it was cured Virginia ham. Hank said that was "pretty damned sophisticated." Hank and Lester were both lean, craggy, and had bad teeth, and she had a hard time getting their names straight to their faces, but they took it good-naturedly, and Lester talked to her about what they hoped would happen, and that the horses'd come over that area beyond the mountain.

When she asked what they were going to do when they did, the men thought that was pretty funny, like she might be thinking they were going to shoot them all, and did she think they were that bad . . . and then Lester (or she thought that was the one who was Lester because of the red kerchief) said all they did was rope them, tag them with this homing sensitizer for the conservation rangers, and take pictures. That it was to keep them alive, not kill'm, and besides that it was a hell of a show and helped their skills for the rodeo.

Then Stan came over with the camera and told her to photograph the tags after they were in place. And then he thought better of it and said "if you want to" which she said was fine, and that was that until he doubled back and added, "You want to try your hand at roping? I'll teach you if you like." But she thought about it and said, "No, I don't feel right about it. I'd rather watch." And he said he'd figured that'd be what she'd say or else he would have offered earlier.

It was very hot, maybe 115—hot enough so she kept putting the block on her face and using the chapstick, but she didn't feel uncomfortable. And she figured a lot of it was just waiting for the horses to show if they showed at all, but Stan didn't seem to mind any of it. Although she could see the heat on him, the line of sweat against the back of his shirt and the half-moons under his arms, and the way he wiped his brow, then looked at her and she at him, but they didn't have to say a word.

When the horses came around the mountain, she counted twenty, and took the binoculars Stan offered. She didn't know they'd be so small, almost pony sized and stocky, not the slim line an Arabian has or even a quarter horse. But they were fast . . . the sand spread out into the air from where they'd been.

Jan was driving the jeep and seemed to know just what to do. Lester was with her, while Billy traded places and got on the dappling, and rode after Hank and Stan. Faye followed, but there was no way the old gelding was going to get up speed, so when she got close enough, she slowed him to a walk and started taking pictures.

Stan roped the leader on a first pass, which was incredible. Even from what Faye knew and didn't know, it was incredible to be able to do that. And she thought she got a great shot of the horse rearing, and one of him pulling him in. The whole thing took half an hour and she thought it was like catching a sailfish on a release. Especially when the fight had gone out of the horse and he could get close enough with the tag gun to clip its ear. Then he cut the line, and there was that second when the horse just stared at him and he at the horse—and all Faye could think of—since she was that way with game fish—was the horse thinking "what the hell you want to put me through all that for and then just let me go?" Lester lassoed a mare from the jeep, and that was interesting as well, although it was his third pass. Still, he made a lot of "whahoos" over it, as did Hank, who got his on the fourth, and that went on for a couple of hours until the men were soaked and the heat wasn't doing anyone any favors, and it made her terribly conscious that she did the same thing fishing—and she felt a little ashamed of the pleasure from the struggle. And didn't realize how tired she was until they'd stopped for a beer in the closest town, and she could barely keep her eyes open.

"I wonder if Ellen went to Phoenix?"

It was close to six and they'd pulled up the long drive to where his ranch was, after the others begged off dinner saying they were too tired and just wanted to have a last beer at the place where they'd been last night.

"You worried?"

"No. Just didn't want any hard feelings."

"It'll be okay. I told her how to get here, and the number. It'll be okay."

"Oh I know it will. It'll be okay."

"You hungry?"

"Very hungry. Oh God, what great doggies! So what are they called?"

"Showdown and Wheatstraw. Hey, Showdown, you old skunk dog. Wheatstraw, he's kinda an orphan—do you want him, Faye?"

"God, what an idea. Do I want him? I don't even know you—I don't know, maybe." Wheatstraw licked her hand, anxious to please.

Showdown wagged his hind-end and panted. Then he lay down before the stone fireplace while Stan put the logs on and started it up.

"Funny how the temperature changes."

"Yup. But no one seems to catch cold."

"Funny."

"Yup."

"May I look around?"

"Help yourself. Bathroom's through there."

Faye took in the house, the books and bookcases and wood beams and dust, and the big, hand-hewn table at one end with rolls of geographical survey maps on it, and the saggy chair she figured was his, and ashtrays everywhere, a

gun cabinet, some medals on the wall, the painting of the
prairie on the longest wall, which she thought was first rate
and reminded her of the nineteenth-century landscapes out
of the Hudson River School; and the bar over at one end
with the bottle of whiskey on it. When she passed through
the bedroom on the way to the john, she felt a little guilty
about her curiosity and looked at the photos on the big roll-
top. Two were of groups, the other a picture of him and a
little girl—the two of them running out of a lake holding
hands and grinning at each other. There was a resemblance,
and she thought she could have cried then if she'd let herself.
But didn't. Used the bathroom instead, and spent a long
time washing her face and hands and prettying herself up.
She swore she wouldn't ask him about the child. And when
she got back, asked if she couldn't do something in the
kitchen.

"Well what do you think?"

"I think you're a man who makes his bed."

"That and the dishes, but not much else. It's a little dusty."

"So's the desert. I'm really starved. It's very 'you,' the
house."

"Yup. It is."

"And I like Showdown. I like Wheatstraw too—he's like
. . . very needy."

"Yah, well they like you too. What about today?"

"I was very happy today. I took a couple of great shots
of you with that lead horse."

"You brought me luck, Slim. I never got one on a first
try."

"That why they didn't come for steak?"

"Maybe."

"Do you want to?"

"Do I want to! From about the first second I laid eyes on
you. Do you?"

"Yes, I want to."

. . . Which was when he kissed her against the refrigerator, and they wound up on the floor in front of the fireplace, and made love with their stomachs growling, and both of them smelling a little rank, and with Showdown looking on mournfully and Wheatstraw wagging his tail, but it was comfortable for both of them and that was the best thing about it. They were both comfortable, even a little awkward and embarrassed they were still comfortable, and it didn't even have to be what it was, and you didn't have to say anything, it was just the hold of it and the little things and it was perfectly comfortable. So that afterwards they slept a little with the blanket from the couch he put over her. And when she woke up he was watching her.

"I promised myself I wouldn't ask."

"Happened ten years ago. She had cancer. I made my peace with it."

"The quality of life not the quantity?"

"Just that. She was one happy kid."

"I'm so sorry, my darling."

"Hey. You're the darlin'. Aren't you the darlin'? Whyn't you roost a little, my darlin'?"

"Roost with you?"

"You got another rooster?"

. . . Which struck them both, and they laughed over that one awhile, just like they had released everything else, except an appetite for food, which seemed the least of it.

"Oh Stan."

"Oh Slim."

"I can't. I've gotta see everything first."

"What happens after you see everything? You reach your girl friend's samadhi?"

"No. I don't know. I never know."

"That's a hell of a way to live—you don't know."

"It's the way I am."

"Love me a little?"

"I love you a lot. So does everybody else. You love me a little?"

"Oh, I reckon."

"Come on, I did first."

"Shore I love you a lot. Probably wind up marrying you, if we got along this good."

"You don't waste time."

"Neither do you. I figure we got a lot in common, but I don't know what. Hey listen, seriously, I'll feel better. Take the dog."

"I'll take the dog—c'mere Wheatstraw. See, he loves me. I'll take the dog."

Then they ate. He cooked up a big sirloin on the grill and she fished around the icebox, and had to settle for boxes of frozen vegetables which she threw together with some butter and white wine and worcestershire, along with some mashed potatoes, and between the two of them, they ate every bit of it. And after that and putting the dishes in the dishwasher, he took a shower and she took a long soak in the claw-foot tub, and they got into bed like it was nothing special, and no matter what she did or didn't do, snuggling into him, with a chill in the air, and the rain starting, she knew she was in love with him, and the hell with Ellen and samadhi.

Two Days and a Hot Tub

The woman said yes she had a cabin available and she did take dogs but she'd have to charge her the full rate, and she was sorry for that, but chances were it would've been taken later on by a couple, so that's the way it had to be, and she was sorry but they didn't take credit cards.

The cabin smelled of pine and had a full kitchenette with dishes but Faye hadn't passed any grocery stores in the last fifteen miles, and it was set up for a family of four with one double bed in the bedroom and two studio couches that doubled, and a kitchenette table before the picture window which overlooked the road and beyond that the valley and next mountain range. It was thirty dollars a night.

"Just be the one night then?" She looked up at her over the turquoise frames, and was about to check one night and receive the money for it.

"I'm not sure, maybe two."

This didn't sit well, and you could tell by the way the woman worried her thumb on her front teeth she didn't feel right about it.

"Been a long day for you, has it?"

"Very long. I started in the middle of Death Valley."

"Nevada! Hell, that's 550 miles."

"I started out at five in the morning."

"What? You camped alone in the middle of the desert!"

"Right. I did. I camped in it."

"My word!"

"Yes, and then I thought I could stay in Yosemite. But everything was full, all the campgrounds and resorts. You were the first place had a room."

"My word."

"And this place looks so pleasant and peaceful. I could really use a rest."

"You come all the way from New York?"

"Well no, the Florida Keys, but my other address is New York."

"Alone? With a tent?"

"Uh huh. I wanted to see the country. Especially the West."

"My word."

She left Faye the key, and three fresh towels, and mentioned the hot tub she had as she was closing the door. As an afterthought, the woman introduced herself as Mrs. Johnson, and called Faye by her first name. "Faye, you need anything just ask my boy for Mrs. Johnson." It was a politeness and an insult and a confusion of what she thought about Faye . . . and Faye figured she might be lonely and want to talk, but didn't trust her yet just the same.

Faye took the first hot shower she'd had in a week and washed out her clothes. The bed, although saggy, felt wonderful. After a month and a half of the ground mostly, it was an odd sensation. She wondered if she might fall asleep for twenty-four hours. But didn't. She felt too good and safe to waste it on sleep.

. . . So she combed her hair and put on a little lipstick and drove the five miles down the mountain where Mrs. Johnson had told her there was a supermarket and a couple of fast food places. She bought what she thought was a great deal of food—a new jar of peanut butter, a hot meatball submarine, potato chips, cookies, a steak, eggs, butter, cheese, crackers, cottage cheese, a ton of dog food for Wheatstraw, and two bottles of California red. Back at her cabin, she washed, clipped, and flea-sprayed Wheatstraw, then cleaned her ice chest and threw out the old peanut butter and cheese which had kept her going through the West. She'd plenty of instant coffee and three cans of condensed milk so that was okay, and enough Coca-Cola and bottled water to get her to China. She put the new stores in the tiny icebox, and opened the wine with her army knife corkscrew. It was quite tasty, a full, mellow Cabernet Savignon, and went well with sitting in the old blue wicker rocker on the porch and looking out at where she'd come from that day.

She'd been through this before. Roughing it and hard driving for a while—or once on a canoe trip in Minnesota where it'd rained for three weeks straight—then getting back to a clean room and store food, how it felt. How wonderful it felt. Hot water and dry clothes and food and the softness of a bed. She felt especially good because of the panic earlier on when she couldn't find any place to stay. And the ranger told her it was all National land and she couldn't camp just anywhere, and she should've made reservations because the parks were all full up on summer weekends and she should try the motels and cabins past where Yosemite ended. Which she did for thirty miles, at every one of them not posting a "no vacancy," and had been turned away. And by that time she was so desert-tired and worn down, her mountain driving was getting dicey and she nearly had a head-on with a Winnebago passing on a sheer drop.

But earlier on, when she was dead center in the middle of Death Valley (late morning, which she took at a hundred and not a soul . . . not one car for four hours, but already a hundred and twenty and the heat waves rising and waving in front of her, and the mirages of lakes in the distance coming one after the other—though she didn't sweat and she didn't feel the heat, and stopped twice to take pictures, and played the radio until there were no stations coming through clear anymore, which was the time she switched on her tape recorder) . . . earlier on but after that, she was in Lone Pine, and it was amazing how the desert ended suddenly, like an ocean shore—and there were all these pines, tall ones and then others which were twisted and stumpy-looking and, she was told, had stood since the day of Christ and were the oldest living trees in existence, which formerly she'd always thought were sequoias. And by that time she'd had it with the desert anyway. There was desert and there was desert. Death Valley wasn't the white pristine dunes of Almagordo. It hadn't the gentle clarity. Death Valley had been like a giant excavation which didn't pan out. It left her feeling desolated and sad—spending the night there, thinking about Ned for courage and Stan because she was in love with Stan. Lone Pine and its fresh doughnuts and chatty owner in the diner came like the grace of God, and after that—going up the mountain to Yosemite, she started to feel tired. Until she got to the park and saw the sequoias and took a little train tour around them. It was like Walt Disney—the hugeness and being surrounded by them. California was a weird state.

. . . So she ate the submarine sandwich and drank some of the Cabernet Savignon, watching the sky change behind the mountains, and felt clean and safe, and got into bed without taking off her clothes and slept twelve hours.

"Sleep well?" Mrs. Johnson spotted her at the pool behind the office.

"Best ever. I needed the sleep."

"I told the boy not to start with the lawnmower til you was up. Gonna stay the extra day?" She was less suspicious now and asked cheerfully.

"Yes, I am. This is a very pretty place you have."

"Well, I've put a lot into it." She said this in a half matter of fact, half sad way, like it had cost her something besides dollars.

Mrs. Johnson left to tell the boy to start the mowing, although Faye had not yet seen the boy, or if he was a boy.

She felt energetic but relaxed and swam laps for the next half an hour while the sun heated up the mountainside and the temperature rose fifteen degrees. But that was something else about being out here. Even the night before last, sleeping in Death Valley, it was one minute a hundred and twenty, and the next fifty, so she was hour-to-hour putting on and taking off clothes, zipping and unzipping her sleeping bag. But that was the desert. This was mountain lush, and the air was wet, chilly and went through you at night, great snuggling weather—and if not Stan, it was nice to have big, fluffy Wheatstraw—who she decided was a golden retriever out of a wolf—keeping her feet warm. And she swam fast in the cold water to get the blood going, but by ten it was hot, and she felt like maybe she'd cook up that steak for breakfast.

"Whew. Hot. Guess you want to get some sun?" Mrs. Johnson stood over her while she squinted up from where she'd been lying. "Been to town and back. Say, you had something to eat?"

"Uh huh."

"I was gonna make lunch, see if you'd like some."

"Thanks, but I stuffed myself."

"Don't look like you stuffed yourself. Wish I could keep a shape like that."

"I dropped ten pounds on this trip."

"On purpose you did?"

"No. I think I just sweat it off in the car. At night, I ate like a truck driver."

"And you did this alone?"

"Uh huh."

"What do you do?"

"I write."

"Oh, that's why you have that typewriter."

"Yup."

"Sell anything?"

"Sometimes."

"Well, I'll tell you, there's a lot of interesting stories about this area."

"I'll bet."

Then Mrs. Johnson went off to fix her lunch, but not before telling Faye to call her Eunice.

Faye thought Eunice handsome in the way big-boned women are. She was medium height, with short, fuzzy gray hair in a halo. She figured they were the same age, and the hair was premature. The mountains had given her a permanent set of red cheeks, and her eyes were phenomenally blue—cornflower blue—and she had sturdy legs, and her upper arms were built up, so Faye figured she'd done a lot of heavy work. When she thought about it, the best-looking feature was her skin color—the ruddy good health—and even the sun-lines of which she had her share looked tight and healthy like a tennis player's, and she figured Mrs. Johnson for someone who had solved a lot of life's problems and was uncomplicated.

"You wanna take a hot tub later on? I'll turn it on if you do." Eunice Johnson had returned from lunch and been giving orders to the boy—who actually *was* a boy—about 18, with straight, dirty blond hair and not a Mexican, which had been Faye's experience with Western white people saying "boy," like Southerner's in the fifties had said "boy" to mean negro helper. "I told the boy to skim the pool for you, he do it?"

"Yes, he did, thank you."

"What about that tub?"

"I've never see a hot tub."

"You never seen one?"

"Well, a jacuzzi yah, but not a real hot tub. Where is it?"

"Right over there, behind the house, you can't miss it."

"That's a hot tub! I thought it was one of those things you get into in bare feet and smash grapes," which broke what was left of the ice to break between the two women, with Eunice holding on to the deck chair while she laughed herself into a teary calm.

"Shoot, Faye. This isn't wine country. Good Lord, I never heard that one before."

"Seriously. It's a wood vat, right?"

"Well, I'm gonna set you up one and you can take it at sunset. How'd you like that? It'll restore you."

"Sounds great. Thanks."

It had been pretty close to a perfect day, doing nothing but getting sun and eating and reading Steinbeck, which was what she thought she should read on her journey, but after a few pages at a time, usually went back to some thriller or other, and around five it started to cool down, with the sun behind the mountain, so she went in, took a shower, and drank the second half of the bottle of Cabernet and chain-smoked Marlboros, and felt good. There were four or five cars parked in front of the cabins, twelve of them she counted—but she hadn't seen many people around. No one had come and used the pool that day. So she figured it was just that Eunice Johnson made a policy of one cabin, one price, and let it go at that. She wondered where her husband was, and if they had children.

"You ready?"

"Uh huh. Aren't you coming in?"

"No. In case someone comes, but I can talk to you."

"That would be nice."

"Water's a hundred and four."

"That hot?"

"But you don't feel it cause the air's cool."

"I would think I'd feel it more."

"No. So you're just traveling around the country. Hope you got a gun."

"No."

"You oughta have a gun. I got one and a rifle. You gotta have one if you don't have a man around."

"Don't you have a . . . ?"

"Heart attack three years ago. But he was quite a bit older."

"Oh, I'm sorry. Kids?"

"Two. Daughter by my third and a son by my first. But not by Harry."

"Harry?"

"The last, the good one, the one who died. I been married four times, Faye."

"You've had quite a time of it."

"You can say that again. But Harry was the best. This place was ours, we threw in our lot together—Harry and me. I was married before to his nephew, all of them lived around here, so he was related to Judy—that's my daughter. He was her great-uncle and her step-father, but he was something—sixty years old and every bit a man. Lemme tell you that's a rare thing."

"Yes, it is." But she wondered what actually a "real" man was that all the women she talked to from all the states and in the Keys and the sophisticated women in New York talked about and how you could define such a thing. Faye had never made her peace with that.

The sun was fading and with it everything—the valley and mountains and the pines—turning violet, and the light softened to apricot while Faye sat in the hot sulphur water feeling the sweat on her forehead grow cold in the chilled air . . . and listened to Eunice, who, once talking, seemed to pour out the bad with the good. This had happened with Faye before—people'd open up and talk about things they didn't normally, because they knew she'd be going away, and whatever intimacy was established didn't seem to hold any price tag to it.

Eunice started with the daughter Judy, getting taken off by a born-again religion and her having to go all the way up to Oregon to get her out—and it was true that they brainwashed her . . . it was true everything they said about those crazy Jesus freaks, and Eunice figured it was the bravest thing she ever did, facing down the people and getting her daughter back, and now Judy was just coming around. This came a year after Harry died, and she was just sixteen, so they had to let her go or the law'd have a case for kidnapping, and it was understandable, given her real father, who, when he cared at all, beat them up over it . . . and her son from her first (his dad moved to Alaska) was the best off of both of them, and damn near killed his step-dad, Judy's father, one night—and then he got out of the charges by enlisting. And she was proud of her boy, who'd just gotten his stripes, she was real proud of him.

"I never would have guessed it, Eunice. I was thinking how healthy and capable you seemed. Like you hadn't had many problems. Someone who'd get a lot of respect in the community."

"Oh well. Now. That's another story. And it's not that I didn't. My people founded this area in the 1840s—that's how far I go back here—so it'd been a good thing, and I guess I've been treated better than most considering what happened. . . ."

But Eunice couldn't tell her just then, because the daughter came out, and said something about going bowling with Charlie, and her mother said that'd be all right if she'd finished with last week's receipts, which she almost had, and Faye thought the daughter might just as well have stayed with the born-agains because unless a miracle occurred, she'd always be a wimp and subject to domination, in the way some pretty girls with dull eyes and round shoulders get dominated.

"She's always gonna have problems, that girl," Eunice sniffed.

"You think so?"

"Well, just look at her. She's got jello for blood. I love her but she's got jello running through her veins."

"She seems very vulnerable."

"She isn't smart either, though God knows I've borne it

. . . since her Dad swiped her one too many, and on the head—and one time . . . I don't know why I'm telling you all this. . . ."

"It's okay, it helps sometimes."

". . . One time he gave her a concussion. Terrible."

"Yes. It says something about your strength that you were able. . . ."

"You think I'm strong, do you really?"

"Yes I do, Eunice, I think you're very strong."

"If you only knew. Oh well."

"You appear very strong, Eunice—full of vitality."

"If you only knew. I got away with it, and then I didn't. Sometimes I just don't know. . . ."

"Don't know?"

"Would you like something to drink. A diet-Coke? I don't have anything hard. I'm sorry but there's nothing hard."

"Oh I wouldn't uh. . . ."

"You sure you're not too hot?"

"I'm very happy . . . you uh, I've some wine in my uh. . . ."

"No, nothing hard."

"Well, it's better not to."

"Yes. I can't. I can't do it anymore."

"No?"

"No."

"Not at all?"

"No. I haven't touched any in. . . . Today's my eighty-ninth day. . . ."

"Eighty-nine days?"

"If I do again, I don't know."

"Oh."

"You said I was strong. If you only knew."

"Yes, you are. Look what you've accomplished. My cabin is spotless."

"Yes, I keep it clean, if I have to do every one myself, and I have—every one."

"Amazing. Twelve cabins."

"And in winter with ice on the mountain. I broke my leg doing it."

"Lord."

"But when Harry was alive, we both did it. God, he was sixty but he was something, every winter we'd go skiing—you should've seen him—best skiier! A kind of natural talent for it—he was practically born on them."

"Oh."

"It's been rough, Faye. I tried to do it with pills once, God help me."

"Terrible."

"And then it was two years of it, but the cops always got me home. I don't think I'll ever forgive myself for neglecting Judy, I know I'm to blame."

"You're too hard on yourself. She's young."

"No. Those bruises don't go away. I can see it in her. First her Dad and then me. . . ."

"You didn't. . . ?"

"No. I never hit her or anything. But the kids in school made her life hell."

"They always do."

"It's a small town—listen, are you sure you're not too hot? I can turn it off. . . ."

"No. I can take a lot of heat. It's divine."

"You know I haven't been in there since Harry died. He's the one built it, hundred percent redwood it is, even the steps . . . and you thought it was a wine vat!"

"It's wonderful, Eunice. You really should start getting in again."

"Oh, you know. It's different when you own one."

"Yes I guess so, still. . . ."

"You should have seen me six months ago."

"What happened . . . or if you don't. . . ."

"No it's okay. I've gone this far—I really don't know why I'm telling you all this."

"Well, it helps. For me too. It gets lonely."

"Oh God. The loneliness. I never thought it was possible."

"I never did, either."

"And I'd always liked to have a good time. . . ."

"Yes, you have so much vitality. I can see that about you."

". . . And after Harry died, and with Judy's problems, I got so I couldn't start off my day without a couple of shots—vodka, I got to drinking it because there wasn't much smell."

"To kill the loneliness?"

". . . And so I could cope. I don't look it but I'm shy. Harry made it so that I wasn't, but after I tried to go out and meet someone and me being shy . . . then all that's left now anyway is the dregs and they want one thing, you know. . . ."

"Right, I know. It can be very tough, especially if you're lonely."

"Terrible, and I woulda settled, but there was nothing to settle for. But I just couldn't get myself to stay home at night. I just couldn't. I couldn't face it."

"Oh Eunice I'm sorry, really. . . ."

"Someone like you, I really admire, I really do . . . you just get up and go. But I couldn't go. This is all I ever knew."

"It's just different that's all. I don't have kids."

"Or a resort. Just a typewriter and paper's all you need, right?"

"Yes I guess."

"I admire you for it. You don't have any kids, do you?"

"No. You asked me that. No."

"Some people weren't meant to."

"No. Some shouldn't."

"Usually they're the ones who do."

"Amen to that."

"I shouldn't have."

"Don't say that."

"I was the town drunk, can you believe it to look at me? God."

"No, I can't."

"Tight dresses and vodka, guess that about says it."

"I can't imagine."

"Crashed two cars."

"Good Lord."

"I was pregnant when I crashed the second. Don't even remember doing it. . . ."

"Doing?"

"Driving. Oh, half the time I didn't remember the other either. There's only one bar in town, I was pretty bad."

"Christ, what a nightmare for you."

"Second time, they tried to take my kids away. Used to throw me in jail all the time just for the night when I got rough. . . ."

"Why'd you stop?"

"Judge ordered me to AA. Gave me a choice of that or taking my kids away and jail. I darn near lost the resort then."

"Well, you look great now."

"I'm just beginning to see things clearly."

"It takes awhile."

"It saved my life. They took care of me, and the pastor at my church found out about it, and he was a big support to me, although I don't go. I don't feel comfortable going. I don't kid myself. If it wasn't for the fact my name goes way back around these parts and I've got family, I think I'd be in jail now. I was lucky."

"Yes. But you were the one who pulled yourself out of it."

"I'm not out of the woods yet."

"I guess it just takes time."

"If I could just get away but I can't."

"Where would you go?"

"I don't know. Lake Tahoe maybe. I always wanted to

go there. Harry and I were planning to but we never did. And I don't know if I could get up nerve enough to go all alone. How do you do it?"

"I don't know. I don't have any family to speak of."

"You're free."

"Yes."

"Scares me to death."

"Me too."

"But in New York, you're never lonely."

"Not in the way you mean. In other ways though. But it must get very lonely up here."

"In the winter when the road gets closed off sometimes, I think I'll lose my mind. But now with this AA, I've made a couple of friends."

"That's wonderful."

"But it's hard getting around with the resort and the distances."

"But your daughter can help."

"Yes. A little. But I can't leave her alone for long."

"You think you might sell it, Eunice?"

"If somebody made me a serious offer I would."

"No offers?"

"Oh I got plenty. From the places closer to Yosemite. You get to know men by their money, Faye . . . every damn one of them tried to rob me. I swear to God, I wish I could live without them . . . you get to know what they're really like."

"Yah, well as a race they leave a lot to be desired. But there's another side to it, Eunice. You're just not seeing it. Or it's not seeing you. . . ."

"Well, I had Harry. I had something once. The rest of them are pigs . . . not all, but most. I'm getting to know one in AA, but we're just friends . . . it's hard, Faye . . . I can see how women get religion when they get older. What else is there?"

"Lots. You're what, forty-two? Fight it. I think you have to view it with boxing gloves."

"I did, but it never worked for me. AA's been a blessing. It saved my life."

"I never would have thought you had a problem to look at you."

"You better get out now, it's been over half an hour. It's bad for you, too much."

That night Faye drank most of a bottle of Cabernet, enough to get a buzz on, and listened to the radio. The whole thing with Eunice scared the hell out of her . . . She figured she had a couple more years on booze, before it turned on her like it did on women when they got past a certain age— and some, like Eunice, before, but most, she thought, after . . . in that time when the men no longer looked twice and the hormones started changing. It was an unholy terror unless you kept busy enough and had good people around you. After a while, even the wine tasted sour, and it was good to know she'd be leaving early.

When It Hit

Wheatstraw barked. And she saw it. And she got that dog back in the car so fast he never knew what hit him. About twenty miles down the road, outside Eclaire, they made camp at the Rest Eazy Campground.

"Got to tell yah we're on a tornado watch."

"I just saw one."

"Where?"

"Driving on 10 in the Badlands."

"You're in the Badlands, honey."

"Well, further back towards Wyoming then."

"You don't say."

He had a nasty look—all skin over skeleton—and warts, one on the side of his nose and the rest at his ears—clusters of them. Flintskin's the name she made up for him. That's the way he came on, and he looked her and her dog up and down.

It was around four. She wasn't hungry yet and the sun was still strong so she and Wheatstraw went swimming. It was a small lake—small enough to be manmade, she wasn't sure—and cold. It dropped off quickly. After she swam and Wheatstraw chased a turtle, she washed and shampooed both of them, and forgot about what she'd seen. It was dusty in the Badlands. Dusty and boring—except Rushmore and the State Park, and a few other things. She missed Wheatstraw's father—her "real" man, her man at the Canyon. She'd phone him later, tell him what she saw—or maybe she shouldn't because then he'd worry—but she was more concerned about the nasty campground manager. There weren't enough others around to keep him in line.

When she got out of the water, Flintskin was watching her, and she tucked a towel around her suit.

"You a gym teacher or something?"

"No. I like to swim."

"Good for a girl to keep in shape when she gets older. You got a real nice shape."

She wanted to kill him—she had this second of wanting to kill him with her bare hands, which maybe she could have done since he was short and skin and bones. It got to Wheatstraw, who lifted his muzzle just a little, and the rumblings of a growl started up.

"He's shy. I better go and feed him."

"You do that, Missy. You need anything, come on in the office."

He smelled of whiskey, and when he walked back to his office, he patted the trunk of her car. She and Wheatstraw looked at each other. He didn't run like she knew he wanted, but stayed so close she felt his wet fur on her leg.

"We better watch that sonofabitch," she said while she was drying him in the old beach towel. They had gone inside a big change-and-shower area for the women, but it wasn't clean, and there were no paper towels, and one of the faucets wouldn't shut off. She felt clumsy all of a sudden, like something sucked all the air out. Wheatstraw lay on the floor and panted.

When they came out, the sky erupted into dark dust. She felt her ears ring and couldn't catch her breath, and she and Wheatstraw ran to the lake and got under the dock—her one hand on the piling, the other around the dog. But it happened so fast all she remembered was grabbing Wheatstraw by the ruff—and then the noise of it—the tearing, horrible wailing—and the funnel she couldn't see until it was beside the lake, and then it was gone.

The first thing that hit her was the smell of gas, and that the air was filled with dirt, but the sun was out again as fast as it had become dark. She wasn't sure how long it took— maybe it was less than a minute, maybe ten seconds. She couldn't get her bearings with time, and everything appeared different. Things like trees and a garage—things she hadn't thought she'd noticed—had disappeared, and she wasn't sure where she was in relation to her tent and the car. But she could follow the line of it. And the smell of gas.

It had hit the ladies shower room, the laundromat—there were machines scattered on the ground—a tree had fallen on a Gulfstream, and the office lay in a rubble of wood.

She went to the Gulfstream first, which had been upended on its door side, so she broke the window, then called out, "Is anybody hurt?" but there was no one inside, and the Gulfstream was the only trailer hit.

All this time Wheatstraw had been whimpering—just before and when it happened—in the water under the dock. Now he was circling the rubble of the office, barking in that kind of high whine that meant both fear and intrusion. Then he came back to her, and pawed the ground.

But she didn't go over there—not then—just leaned against the trunk of her car, and felt peaceful.

There were some clothes, a small wood carving, a car resting against a tree with its axle side up, the washers and dryers, a chair, a steering wheel, and then she saw a white angora cat—the kind that had been coddled as a housepet— stuck through on the high end of a television antenna that had been downed. It was still alive, mewing horribly with its mouth drawn back over its fangs, the claws stretched and grasping. She took the wet towel she still had around her shoulder and wrapped it around her hand to pull the thing free—but part of the stomach and intestines were spilled— and she knew she should kill it quickly, but didn't know the best way. She tried with a board and it didn't work, so she put the towel over the cat and broke its neck with her hands. Then she was swearing and crying with the feel of it still there, but that passed.

All the while she'd been killing the cat, Wheatstraw had stayed beside the collapsed boards of the office, although he no longer barked, and she took her time going over.

It wasn't big or anything. Just a cabin with the front part for reception, a registration desk, the usual mailslots for keys, a television mounted so people could watch from the sofa or the few chairs around—a couple of plastic philodendrons prettying up the place. There was a room behind the reception area, which when she had checked in, she figured was where Flintskin stayed, or maybe it was two rooms. She saw then that it must have been. The gas seemed to be coming from there. She worried for a minute—looking around at all the wood—it might explode.

There wasn't much problem picking through—hauling what was left of the boards, throwing them to the side until she could get to him. Part of an arm sticking through the rubble which she'd seen from the first—from right after when they'd looked over at it. So it wasn't much to uncover him—dead— part of his skull flattened—one eye hanging, the other one giving her that same damn fish stare, which was about as gruesome as she'd wished it—when she wished it . . . al- though he would have been just as dead anyway. Even so, she'd learned something about herself that day. And it was just as well, the cops showed up when they did, so all she had to do was feed her dog, and answer their questions.

What Kind of Man

The first place they stopped was the flea market off
23, but it was too beautiful a day to get serious over cheap
lamps, so they spent less than ten minutes looking at 1940s
brass, then walked out back to where the high grass started
beside the railroad track.

The last of the cornflowers were blooming in straggled
bunches and there were goldenrod, black-eyed susans, and
those purple clusters of daisies. It was sixty-two degrees, and
yesterday in the city they got sideswiped by what was billed
as the biggest hurricane of the century—which didn't come
off, but there'd been white caps splashing over the retaining
walls of the Hudson and the wind got up to eighty, and
New Yorkers went out into it, and were especially friendly
with each other. And they had gone so far as to tape the
picture windows and pull the blinds in front of them, move
the rugs to the front of the apartment, fill the tub, and
prepare for the impossible, which everyone knew wasn't going
to happen—and didn't—or did—but not as much as everyone
feared, though they didn't believe it as they feared it.

So after that, they just took off into the Catskills, because
he hadn't seen anything out of Manhattan, and as a Western
country man, she wanted him to know that New York wasn't
New York but something else.

The maples were already showing red at the tips and the

autumn mushrooms ringed the meadow behind the auction and flea market barn. They figured they were about thirty miles out of Woodstock, and here it was with the sun shining, the air smelling of early fireplace fires, skunk, and manure. He went and got their sweaters from the trunk of the car, and then they walked down alongside the track until they came to a path leading into a bank of trees with a fast-running stream between them.

"She didn't really say that, did she?"

"I told you, she did."

"But that's stupid. It's stupid to say such a thing."

"It's Ellen, and the city mentality, and my having you. She said just the opposite when she met you at the Canyon. Ellen is dropped forever from my roster of friends."

"Even so, Slim, it'd be the same saying something like that any place, not just your fancy salon—any place it'd be the same damn thing."

"But I think you take it too seriously."

They were sitting on a rock alongside the stream, where the sun broke through the tree tops and warmed them so they took off their sweaters and sat there leaning into each other, with his arm around her. She was thinking of the last year—him, the trip, the book—the once-a-month flights back to Arizona, loving him, knowing it'd need work. She'd lose him. She couldn't be what she had to be with him. Then the whole thing about the operation.

"Damn. You know. This is the first time that I can breathe."

"I know."

"I even thanked God for the storm."

"Because it made the city be like the country for a while."

"I'm not made for this, Faye. Jesus, I still can't believe she'd say something that stupid."

"Well, it's not true, darling. If I took it seriously, I wouldn't have said anything about it to you. I thought you'd think it was funny."

"Where I come from, you say something like that about a man, he Goddamn near kill you and get away with it."

"It's meaningless here. People think differently."

"You couldn't get me to live there for love nor money."

"Not even for love?"

"You know what I mean. And it kills that."

"I told you."

"You said you needed me."

"I know. I said don't come and then I said I needed you. But it's over. I did what I was supposed to do, and we can go."

"But it's beautiful here."

"Yes. I haven't been up in ten years and it seems more beautiful than I remember."

"It *feels* good."

"Real."

"Yes, real. You know, we haven't—since the first night we got in."

"Three weeks and two days."

"Well, at least you counted, Slim."

"Well, you didn't want to either."

"I felt uncomfortable."

"Because of all the attention I got? It's just business. Lasts fifteen minutes, that's what Warhol said."

"It didn't smell right."

"I know."

"You need it though. You'll have to go there sometimes."

"Yes, when I have to. It's complicated."

"I feel like I can't be 'right' with myself there."

"That your rules don't apply?"

"I don't know. You were a stranger, Faye."

"But I love you."

"It was stronger than that."

"Did that guy—that friend of Ellen's . . ."

"No, are you kidding. He just went on about art and bars and cowboys—I wanted to deck him."

"We haven't much time put in, that's all—and she knows it. She wants to stir it up. She's a despoiler and an unhappy woman. So please don't talk that way."

They saw a herd of deer, maybe a dozen—which reminded her of being back at the Canyon—when she'd first met him and had stopped on the way . . . a stag with a full set of antlers standing on the other side of the stream. They stopped talking and watched for a while, until he got wind of them and drew himself up, then ran back into the trees with the others following.

"I can't believe this is here."

"It's all around us."

"But it's only four hours to the city."

"The 'City' is a state of mind, Stan. It's only twenty miles, if you include the boroughs."

"But it's the world, right?"

"It's not our world. This is our world."

"I think I could live here, Faye. I think I could spend some time."

"Let's spend some time."

"Let's you 'n me seriously look around. I mean drive it. It's just so Goddamn good being here."

"I know it is, Stan."

"Member that hotel we passed?"

"The one that we said looked like something out of The Waltons?"

"You said that."

"All right, I said that. Let's stay there. What do you say?"

"Why not. After we drive around."

"Right."

They took as many little roads as they could and got lost and walked down to different streams or maybe it was all the same stream only miles away, and they stopped at the Lion's Den Lounge for lunch where they ate hamburgers and he drank Coors, she had a glass of milk at the bar and shot some eight ball on the old quarter machine with the rough felt. Then she asked directions and took him to a little waterfall she remembered outside Palenville, and they found puffballs and boletus, and on the trees some good oyster fungus, and they used her mushroom book and she wondered if instead of the Walton motel they might want to find a cabin with a kitchen so they could cook up the mushrooms and she'd show him how.

He'd gone along with the cabin idea, said he'd preferred it, and they found one—lucked into it—which was more a lodge than cabin, but with a kitchen, and they'd bought a steak and a six-pack, milk, some butter for the puffballs, and fried them up in cracker meal, and everything was out of this world—because they were happy again. And it was as if New York City had disappeared.

But it had done something to them just the same—she could see it in the way they were with each other—their formality with one another—his defensiveness . . . and she promised herself she'd never bring him there again. She'd get out—she'd give up her place, and only come in for her books. Or maybe she'd just sublet the place because where would she go when she had to come in? . . . and how often would that be? . . . once a year? . . . for a week, maybe? . . . could she do it in a week? . . . was everything tied to the city? Lots of writers weren't. She figured it was more complex than that—it had more levels—her independence maybe— or an anonymous refuge for the single life when she'd been single. But he was more important than that. More important than all of it. Except she loved it there—being there when she could walk every neighborhood—and the restlessness, and the variety. But it had cost them. She felt it here, too— and it was true—in the city she didn't much want to be close to him. Maybe it was the book coming out. Or maybe just the last year and a half of her flying back and forth to the Canyon, the two worlds of her loving him. Or maybe it was the way he was feeling that she could feel—a disjoint-edness—like they were slipping away. But that was over and so was the storm. Besides, what she had to tell him was so important. It was a kind of miracle for her. And here they were and they could be here for a day or a week before they went back West. Although from the way he was talking she wondered how tied he was to the Canyon and his ranch. She didn't care as long as they were tied to each other.

They were sitting on the steps of the lodge watching the night and eating Snickers. The sky was full of stars, and he ticked off the constellations, and told her the differences between the way the stars looked here and how they appeared over the Canyon. But he wasn't homesick. He made a point of telling her that. And they both felt like they could stay here together.

"Why did she say that, Slim?"

He was driving her crazy with it.

"Stan. You didn't listen to what I said. She didn't say *you were*. She said, you were too good to be true, and was I sure—*you weren't.*"

"Yah, but to think it."

"Oh Christ. She's a frustrated city girl. She doesn't know anything. Besides she was attracted to you, I could tell."

"You could tell?"

"She's always attracted to the guys I . . . oh shit."

"What am I, one in a list?"

"No. Listen, this is ridiculous. Men I dated when I was single, that's all. Normally she likes pretty boys. Please, Stan, sweetheart, let's forget New York. We're done with it. Do you like the book?"

"Your book?"

"Yes, my book."

"Yes. I'm proud of you. I liked it."

"You didn't. I know you didn't."

"Yes I did. I don't understand all of it, but I like it."

"What don't you understand?"

"Why there's so much sex in it."

"I don't know why either. It's the way I write."

"I don't like that my woman says that stuff."

"But it's in a book not in our life."

"It's in your life all right."

"I won't write about it anymore then."

"No. That wouldn't be right either—Faye?"

"What?"

"I'm scared I can't keep you happy."

"Don't say that. I told you, New York's weird."

"But it isn't just the city. It's you. And the life, what makes you move."

"I know. But the book's out. I don't have to be there. I'm content. You brought me something. You resolved something."

"I don't know that you don't have to be there."

"Well, I don't, Stan. What I really want to do is learn how to take care of the ranch and write. Please. Okay?"

"It's hell four months of the year."

"So it's rough."

"It wouldn't be so rough if we did it here."

"No, it wouldn't be so rough. But the other's your home."

"I can be a lot of places."

"All I care about is us being together."

"Then why were you like *that* in the City?"

"Like WHAT, Stan?"

"I don't know."

"Phony?"

"Yah. A little."

"I don't even think of it like that anymore. It's just the skin you have to put on to survive. It's like putting on an astronaut suit when you're thrown out in space. If you don't have it secure, you can't breathe and you die."

"I don't want to lose you."

"Nor I, you."

It was cold, and the bed sagged and there was only the space heater, which the owner apologized for, but he said this was the last week of being open anyway. They closed for the winter and had a mobile home in Sarasota. Maybe the cold and the bed helped, but they would have been close no matter what the conditions were, and it was good—the way it was before coming to the city, and they lost all of that resentment. She could tell he felt more in control. He was getting his bearings back now, and it was dumb of her to tell him what Ellen said. When she thought about it honestly, she probably told him to enlist his contempt of her "former" friend—that he'd see it as a kind of black joke and think it in some odd way funny.

"You awake?"

"Barely. Let me put my feet on your back."

"Seriously, why'd that woman say that?"

"Jesus Christ, will you stop, Stan! Because you're better, because you're more worthy in my eyes—because she's a competitive bitch, because it was my moment for a change and not hers. Now will you give it up? I love you. What time is it?"

"Five o'clock."

"Oh honey, God. Go to sleep. Here, put your hand here, and go to sleep."

"I can't sleep. You sleep. I'll take a walk."

She was awake by then, and she knew he didn't want her to go back to sleep, and Venus was clear on the horizon through the windowpanes.

"You know part of what was wrong, Stan?"

"What?"

"You felt like my wife, like you had to follow me around."

"I felt like I was a lazy bum, that's the way I felt."

"I can understand that. But you don't know what it was to have you there—just to know you were there, part of me. I needed you."

"You did? You didn't act like you did."

"Well, I did."

Later they went and found a diner that advertised hunters' breakfast specials, and after they finished it was only eight so they drove around Hudson and down to Saugerties, and took in the Ashokan Reservoir, which was down to draught conditions, and she explained how the reservoir, up to this year, serviced all of Manhattan. And then he stopped at a real estate office outside Cairo, and asked about property available.

"Why are you doing this, Stan? You don't want to move East."

"Why not? Why don't I?"

"Because the Canyon's your home. It's always been."

"Well, it's not *your* home."

"It is now."

"But you'll have to go into New York."

"Stop worrying about New York."

"Well it isn't just that, anyway."

They'd been walking along the Sleepy Hollow trail, mushrooming for a couple of hours. It was mostly little paths offset by meadows, the occasional stream, and you could tell there was some human management of the forest parts here. Before that, taking the turn from Phoenicia, up past Chichester and Lanesville and taking the turn on 23A, they'd passed a Rip Van Winkle bridge, a Rip Van Winkle Antiques, even a Rip Van Winkle Auto Body.

"Kahnda cutsy on the Van Winkles. I take it Washington Irving came from here."

"I guess."

"I used to read his stories all the time when I was a kid."

"You read a lot, Stan. I've noticed that about you."

"Hell, yes. There wasn't any TV, and we didn't get but one radio station."

"Were you poor?"

"No. But we weren't rich. My Dad was well thought of in the business."

"Horses?"

"Horses. We had the best ranch north of Phoenix."

"Then why are we looking at spreads in the Catskills?"

"Don't you want to?"

"Yah. I love it. I mean I love looking at places with you, and it's beautiful."

"Faye, I don't have to be at the Canyon all the time."

"Your life is there."

"Well, yours is here."

"No, it isn't."

"You know what I mean."

"Yah, okay, maybe."

"This is great country, Faye. Great country."

They were back at the Lion's Den. Before it'd warmed up to the high sixties but now with dark settling in it was down to where they could see their breath. They decided to stay a couple more days and look around, though both of them had taken to a thirty-acre spread with six meadows, a pond, and a stream. The price was cheap enough. Although Faye felt he might regret it. And she thought the real estate agent just about put it all on the line for him, and Faye felt she had reason to feel jealous. But women naturally took to him. Men too. She wished the agent had been a man, and less into the hard sell—and pushing her thigh against his in her Mercedes. When she said that to Stan, he said, "Oh, they all do that, that's why they're in that line of work—just like those guys fawned all over you," which went completely over her head, and she found him a little small-minded in his reasoning.

"You really think you might want us to spend some time up here?"

"Maybe."

"They've got a lot of horse farms in New Jersey. Colts Neck, White House, places like that."

"I've been there. Race horses mostly. Know something?"

"What?"

"No reason why we couldn't have both—East and West."

"Can we afford it? I could sell the house in the Keys."

"No. We want that too, don't we. We could rent it the rest of the year."

"Yah, we could do that."

"The point is, Faye, we could do anything within reason, as long as we know where we stand."

"Yes, that's true."

"So's the marriage on again?"

"Will you ask, please."

"I thought I did."

"No, you never exactly asked."

"Well, will you?"

"What, will I what?"

"Marry me—Jesus Christ, you're the big libber—we're s'posed to do this by mutual consent—come to think of it, you never damn well asked me. Okay, will you marry me?"

"Yes."

"And would it be okay to have a ranch in the Catskills?"

"Yes, it would."

"And then you'd be closer to the City."

"But you're not doing it for that alone, are you?"

"No. Because this is right. This is it, Faye. It's beautiful here. A man can breathe here."

They ate at the Lion's Den, and Stan drank enough Jack Daniels to get himself flushed, but it was just around the bend in the road from the lodge. And this time there was the beginning of a frost on the windowpane. And after they decided that they'd buy the thirty-acre spread they saw, and that they both felt the same way about Durham and Palenville and the little roads around there—after they agreed that it was necessary for both of them to feel like they aren't forced out of their element, she told him she was seven weeks pregnant. What she'd waited to tell him because of all the boloney about the book, and New York, and Ellen. And when she told him, it was five in the morning again, and they were both wide awake with her feet on the backs of his thighs. And he just laughed and said, "Well, you just tell that to that silly dame—you just tell her what kind of a man loves you."

&
OTHER
STORIES

Clean and Gentle Moments

"I got this crazy notion to. . . ." He says it like it's no big deal his being here, and she wasn't half-scared to death with the storm and his face all mashed in the wind, and her already knowing what he did. But it's not like she could stop him coming in.

"Oh Jeez, Frankie, you gotta get outa here."

"How's that?!"

"Come on . . . they're looking for you."

Now that was really something! Wasn't that something—a Goddamn hurricane and her just standing there telling him that. "Hey I got a notion to . . . how come you run out on me, Sue Lynn?"

"I din't. You scared me."

"You deserved it."

"Maybe I figured weren't no end to it, and it was a sign."

"Sign! What sign? You deserved it."

"Listen, no kidding, you gotta get out."

"I got this crazy notion to. . . ." He saw how scared she was, and took some feeling in it—like he'd been scared and excited breaking out. And he truly believed it was God brought him here. He truly believed it, not her saying about the Keys before. No, it was good her being scared—all those branches flying round out there—and the water. Jesus, she was some piece, even scared!

"Quit! Quit it, Frankie!"

"Hey, you know how it is."

"No, jeez, listen . . . you gotta help, okay? Okay Frankie? Tape them glass doors so's I can. . . ."

She couldn't even get the tape right. She had it all stuck together, and he had to get it right—but it was nice—nice taping the sliding glass doors—couldn't even hold on to hating her. Not rightly. Something . . . baby powder . . . her always smelling of baby powder . . . all that soft baby talk so he couldn't barely hear her til he got used to it only now her screaming with the TV antenna blown clean from the wires. Oh man, he should crush her. She was so bad and all he wants is to touch her . . . couldn't cut the feeling from him even after what went down. . . . Weird! . . . weird purple light of the storm . . . getting his thinking weird . . . he liked it. He liked the antenna crashing and the plants flying round because it kept her scared.

"Jeez, I hate not knowing."

"Not knowing what . . . what, Sue Lynn?"

"Not knowing how bad it's gonna get. What you do anyway?"

"Nothing. I didn't do nothing . . . he had three days of coke in him and he come for me, and all I done was hit him one harder. That's the honest to God truth!"

"I heard it you kill't him."

"He kill't hisself."

"Oh Lord, you better leave, Frankie. You don't understand . . . no really, it's bad. You gotta go, Frankie—please! For me! Pleasepleaseplease?"

"Hey, you look real pretty all sunburned . . . you do, you look real good."

"Oh please Jesus, just leave. . . ."

"Here . . . you got the damn board upside down . . . hey, Sue Lynn . . . Sue Lynn, let me do it. Oh man! Twister! Damn . . . you believe that!"

Big old banyan went clean over with its toes in the air

. . . funny . . . "toes in the air" . . . "lots of purple air and lots of toes in her hair" . . . she knew how scared she was 'cause she started rhyming in her head, and he thinks she's holding on to that damn board just to prove something. But it weren't that little waterspout scared her . . . just give him a line . . . give him a line and make up your mind . . . If she could figure a way to get to Clancy's before he came and got her . . . jeez, she had time . . . cops hadn't even got the mobiles evacuated. . . . Oh please Lord, let me marry Clancy . . . let me be a good police wife . . . please don't let him find out . . . see, it'd all make sense . . . please, I don't want to go back, thank you Lord Jesus . . . shit, she might as well just die if he found out. So it didn't matter, and the praying made her strong. She figured she could shoot him if she had to.

"Hey, we did okay, you and me, Sue Lynn."

"Listen, I got money. I'll help you."

"Slow down woman. You got company coming?"

"Like who?"

". . . Got a nice place here . . . real nice."

"Ain't like it belongs to me, you know that . . . see, I got this job minding houses . . . ain't like it belongs to me, Frankie."

"Oh yah, they told me at the Tiki, that's how I knew to find you . . . ain't that right, Sue Lynn . . . bartender always did know where you at . . . huh . . . said you was into a cop too . . . said you got a real nice deputy . . . he own you now?"

"No way. Uh uh, nobody owns me. Nobody ever owns me."

"Maybe I own you, and I ain't leaving."

"Aw don't talk like that. I hate it when you talk like that . . . the water's got under the door . . . pleaseplease, I'm scared. Get the rug, Frankie, we can talk about that stuff after."

Now she knew the answer . . . just keep him doing stuff

. . . let him help her with the rug. Please Jesus, don't let there be a tidal wave thank you . . . she couldn't even see the dock for the water . . . higher than her maybe . . . still, she had time to get to Clancy's, and she'd do anything for that . . . and maybe she could make Frankie feel they'd be together if he went, and maybe he turned her on, and maybe she still had it for him. So what.

"Hey darlin, where's Rogue? Where's my Roguey?"

"Oh jeez, Frankie, I'm real sorry. Didn't they tell you? I'm real sorry."

"Aw no . . . not Rogue . . . not my Rogue dog . . . aw shit, Sue Lynn."

"He just ran out y'know . . . I'm real sorry."

"No you ain't . . . you let him loose, didn't you, didn't you. . . . Goddamn! That was my Rogue, that was my Goddamn good dog."

"Hey! You're the one got busted."

"For nuthin'. . . ."

"That's bull. That is, Frank . . . you got forty thou."

"Yah, and you got me that sucky lawyer . . . aw Rogue, Jesus, Rogue. . . ."

"But you shouldn't a fought back. They held that against you."

"Yah, and you just took off for the Keys. Oh, you really loved me a lot, a whole fucking lot, Sue Lynn! Aw Rogue . . . Rogue boy."

"I did. I did love you a lot. Jeez, Frankie, lay off that . . . please . . . don't get all wasted . . . you can't . . . please . . . we still got them windows . . . we'll get wasted after . . . okay . . . okay, Frankie? You know how you get . . . jeez, you wouldn't a got busted if you wasn't wasted . . . please, honey. . . ."

. . . Like she didn't booze as much as he did, but God he knew blind it'd be in the fridge door—who'd a heard of keeping whiskey in the fridge door. She was weird about little things like that . . . keeping that little bottle of perfume

stuff right next to it . . . right there in the center. He liked
it she hadn't changed . . . that he knew her mind real good
. . . like she had this horny, trashy way about her sometimes
what made him crazy . . . doing it . . . like she was made
out of cocaine . . . a real sweet badness. Oh Lord, let Sue
Lynn and me go back to the way it was before—it was good
before—her and me had real clean, gentle moments when
we first was in Georgia and fixing up the mobile . . . Lord,
we was decent—you know we was decent—Please God . . .
he hated to think it . . . even when he should hate her . . .
he hated to think it . . . them being broke and the truckers
knowing and him not knowing and her doing it behind his
back . . . worst that could happen . . . hurting her bad
didn't give him no relief neither . . . hell, he didn't need
much, just her and the trailer and Rogue . . . funny, he
knew Rogue for dead even before her telling him . . . he
knew . . . like he knew her doing it, and him fighting with
her not to, got him in the Business . . . drugs fucked him
sure as she did. But she was right . . . she did try and cover
him on the bust, and he couldn't rightly hold what happened
in the bar against her . . . Lord, make it go back to before,
make it decent and clean again.

"Frankie, I'm real scared."

"Huh?"

"I mean it. I'm just shaking all over."

"Yah, you are . . . hey! gimme one of them hard hugs,
Sue Lynn, c'mon now."

"Oh jeez, Frankie, you got some timing."

Now lightning was different. That scared him . . . the
other didn't . . . that big, jagged silver and the sky like a
devil's skeleton . . . but he couldn't show her it scared him
. . . he'd hold her real tight and pretend it don't bother
him . . . stop thinking like a kid . . . he knew, he'd think
it out . . . it was his grandma's telling him scripture with
the lightning . . . filling his head full of electric chairs and
he was going to fry if he were bad.

"Oh Frankie, that was nice, that was real nice."

"That was, that really was, uh huh." Man, she was something! Right on the floor . . . didn't even make it to the bed . . . just slam bam . . . the way she wanted it too . . . them being scared and the storm . . . he knew she felt it too . . . just his little girl all curled up side him.

"You still got time, Frankie. You could make it to Key West. Clancy gonna come and find you, Frank."

"You're crazy . . . he don't know 'bout us?"

"No."

"Well, fix it. You got that cop round your finger."

"You quit! I do not."

"You do. I know'd you but it don't matter. Hey . . . the way I look at it, it's us like before, Sue Lynn . . . and nothing else matters, so we gotta do what we gotta do."

"I know." . . . Please Lord, make him go . . . even it feeling better with Frank . . . but she figured she could do with anybody and it didn't make no difference. Clean money, respect made the difference . . . she could do it! . . . she had to do it! . . . feels real calm . . . even with the storm . . . real calm . . . real strong.

"Listen Frankie, I'll go with you. We'd have to go someplace else but I got enough."

"Go to Nevada like we used to talk about?"

"Sure."

"Want to?"

"Yah, I want to."

"What about the cop?"

"He don't matter."

It was something . . . knowing you were meant for each other and being together . . . like he fit with her, and the Lord made one for one and that was it . . . so peaceful . . . him feeling this peacefulness all at once . . . lightning didn't bother him none ever . . . funny . . . the lightning and most hurricanes he knowed didn't have much . . . and this one being everything at once. But now he liked looking through the boards at the trees and the water over the dock, and the lightning. It was beautiful. He wasn't scared and it was beautiful . . . just this peace—real clean, gentle peace . . . just now, like him and Sue Lynn at first, and the guy being killed didn't happen or her doing what she did. Man, it was the world turned you . . . not you that turned you.

"Hey, where you going?"

"The john, while we still got water. Whyn't you see if you can board up them window spaces. Hey! . . . I gotta go bad, Frankie, okay . . . c'mon honey, quit . . . don't you trust me . . . quit, c'mon, you know me . . . I always gotta go after."

She had a nice back. Nice, long neck and shoulders, nice back to her legs, real tiny ankles, a lot of bleached blond hair over the brown hanging down her back . . . from the back she was beautiful . . . from the front she was okay except her nose was squashed a little and she had acne scars on her cheeks . . . he loved her from the back . . . doing it . . . like loving up a movie star or something . . . even if it was a sin to think it . . . her with that funny sway going through the bedroom to the john . . . and he just wanted the peacefulness a little longer before he got to the boards . . . even though this last gust shakes the house so hard he can't think straight . . . and she's taking too long . . . but she always took too damn long, or maybe she tricked him, but he didn't believe it . . . just peaceful . . . seeing it in his mind . . . real clear . . . one of them double-wide mobiles with a deck, and he figured maybe a gas station real close to the desert . . . all clean and decent and open . . . and a couple a new Rogues . . . and kids . . . being close to the Lord again . . . and her making him chili . . . he could almost smell it. Shit, he was in hog heaven, he was . . . even if there was no sense to it . . . that was the weird part . . . him feeling this peace with the guy being dead, and them looking for him . . . Please Lord, make it true . . . I'll be the best I can for you Lord, please make Sue

Lynn and me purified . . . like his Grandma saying—"Scripture True." Grandma, I do truly believe, sweet Jesus. Now he knew . . . it was the storm purified them same as fire . . . him and Sue Lynn been blessed and forgiven and made holy by the storm. He truly believed it a little . . . God's promise if they got through it. He knew she felt it too, and it was going to be all right.

The Beach at Manuel Antonio

Parts of the beach at Manuel Antonio are full of high rocks and parts are long stretches of smooth sand. And sometimes the jungle touches the beach but usually you have to climb and then take a path to it. From any elevation you can see a mile out to where the Pacific dips into the Bay then slams into three huge boulders right at the shoal line sending a geyser of spume that on sunny afternoons appears red and crimson before it passes through the arch in the highest rock. Once past the shoals, the water calms and turns a greenish blue then flows to shore so gently you can walk a long ways out before hitting a wave.

At the beginning of where the sand turns white and the rocks give way to dunes, there's a small bar—no more than a tin-and-thatch hut open to the sea, with a few cracked stools, half a dozen tables, and its proprietor—Juan Cordova—is a poet who for the price of a glass of the cheap local, "tinto," will happily sit down and drink with you. Other than Juan's and except for the hotel which wasn't on the beach and had no bar, there was little else until you got to the village and that was a rugged six miles away.

The man and woman liked this stretch of Costa Rica best. They liked the beach and the rice and banana fields, the high palms, the jungle nature of it, the tiny hamlets run by the plantation *sobrestantes,* the Indian faces of the "Ticos" walking the sides of the pitted coastal road under their broken straw hats and open white shirts—and always a machete held loosely by the side of their hip or worn in a leather sheath from the waist. Sometimes they carried rifles, which at first made her nervous. But the rifles were for shooting down the high bunches of coconuts and for boar, or more often for snakes which were common and poisonous although a good Tico could cut the head off a bushmaster with his machete from thirty paces, or that's what Juan Cordova said.

The food in the little hotel was plain but quite good—camarones from Puntarenas, eggs, sopa de polla, fish, and plantain. Everything was flavored with cilentro, which dominated the taste, and one escaped the sameness with hot peppers and cold beer. It was a pleasant, peaceful place.

Some mornings the man and woman would rise at daybreak, around six, and take the path over to where the jungle began. They would have to walk across a boggy area coming in from the sea that at low tide held no water and at high tide came above their knees. On one such crossing, when the tide was at its fullest, she had seen a large snake, which swam too close and panicked her. But the man had not seen it, and only remarked it must have been a broken tendril from one of the banyans. After they'd gotten across and looked back at how the current had swirled to an eddy, and where the tide had risen over the top rushes, she started to cry. They could have drowned for his foolishness she said, and the muck from the bottom was clinging to their legs and stank of decay, and furthermore he'd hurt her not believing what she saw, and it was a point of honor between them. When he understood this, he held her and whispered he was sorry—that he would never hurt her—that she was his whole life to him—and why didn't they go over to Juan's and get a little high and listen to him recite his awful poetry on the beach. She agreed, and later thought what a fine man he was—and good to her—and sometimes full of courage although he let people take advantage of him, and it made her sad that she could not love him the way he loved her.

Today, a week later they started early into the jungle again, and this time they had checked the tides to know when to cross. What they did was climb around the rocks and up the little pathways where they could view the orchids and toucans, and from one high place, a ravine with a waterfall where sometimes there were monkeys. Then they climbed down closer to the shore and rounded the point, which was the farthest they'd been, and walked maybe a mile beyond before spotting a patch of beach below. The beach was surrounded on three sides by rocks, some jutting a ways into the water, and she thought perhaps there might be caves, but if not they would soon be hungry, and she'd packed a lunch of bread, goat cheese, and the local preserved ham, which tasted like a spicy prosciutto and went well with the sharp tang of the local wine. They decided to climb down.

When they found the smoothest part of the sand, she spread out a blanket and took the food and wine from their trailbag while the man went to search the back rocks. But there were no caves, only pools of water, and since neither were hungry, they decided to take a swim. The beach was wider than it had seemed from above, and the openness of it—after they were naked and racing each other into the water—freed her into a kind of wild happiness, as if there were nothing else but what they had within the boundaries of the rocks or as far as they could go in the sea—farther than at Juan's—deeper—the sand underfoot packed firm— and the weight of the first roll of wave when they dove into it—and the cooler water—prickled their skin and felt delicious. After a while they floated down the beach on the current, then when they were too tired to swim anymore, sat at the edge of the shallows and let the swells knock them over.

They thought it was the most beautiful day they'd ever seen, a chance breeze and the temperature no more than eighty, the horizon boundless, the surface of the water glistening with sunbeams, and behind them vines of allamanda and passion flower spilling over the rocks . . . and the only sounds—those of the surf and the gulls and from time to time the staccato shrill of monkeys high up in the banyans.

It put her in a mind to try and love him back the way he loved her. If she could do this—if she could control and direct it—then perhaps there would be some peace. Because in the past she'd loved badly—the kind of men who were made of fire but with little heart and no honor and had shown no simple kindnesses to others. They had pursued her until she loved them back, and then it was only a question of power. But this man flowered with a different kind of strength, and they were in a beautiful place, and he had taught her to trust him. . . . So if she could learn not to want the fire anymore—if she could change it to be with him the way he was with her—then it would be all right. She knew it would be all right.

Still, she shut her eyes and endured it—though why she couldn't say. He was a generous lover—no less knowledgeable than any of the others . . . and she thought halfway into it, she might be beginning to change—that it was an opening for her—that all the time when he had begun, slipping his arm around her waist with this faint "con permiso" in his eyes and her half-contemptuous "yes," she had been praying— that she was at first begging God that it should be so, but that now she was no longer begging but admitting she had no control and never did . . . and it was then, in her failing and when she had given up . . . she felt some sort of pleasure. And though it wasn't great pleasure, since it wasn't an abandon or anything like that . . . still, there was some measure of peace in it, and she was grateful for that.

On her back she could watch the movement of the birds, the high mare's tail clouds—she could observe the heliconias growing out of crevices in the rocks, and the sun and periwinkle sky . . . and she could tell him he made her happy, and tell the truth that he did . . . until he could sense the difference and believed her . . . so that later, his face when she held it in her hands looked almost luminous, like one of those Sunday School pictures of Saint Francis.

Afterwards, they took a long time eating and drinking, then swam again to work off the languor . . . and emerged from the water laughing and full of light talk and energy, deciding that what they should do was to go hear Juan Cordova read some more of his poetry . . . and take pictures of him with the sunset in the back . . . and have his bar boy take pictures of the three of them together.

Juan Cordova stood up from the barstool when he saw them coming, shook the man's hand but only bowed to the woman, and smiled with the one front tooth missing, the other gold, and made like they were his dear friends and he hadn't seen them for years. Which was the way it always was after they'd drunk a few glasses of "tinto," and tasted the "bocas" of cilentro, rice, and tidbits of fried fish the bar boy put out. Then Juan rubbed his stomach, picked up the legal ledger, walked out on the beach, and began to read his latest poem, which was about love and the beach at Manuel Antonio. It was a terrible poem even with their limited Spanish, full of sentimental excess and going on for a good ten minutes, after which they applauded and yelled bravo. . . . And which, despite the fact it was terrible, seemed almost transcendent for the life he put into it—the performance redeeming the words and with his whole body in play, not just the hands. He would pace the beach, hold up the open ledger, sweep his other arm full around, pause, grimace, fall to his knees, grow a tear to where it coursed down one cheek, then laugh and howl.

After he had finished the poem, he asked if they knew of any American publishers who might be interested. He always asked this in some form or other because they were both writers, and he felt sure they'd understand. And they always explained they were "periodistas" and wrote only about current events, and didn't know about poetry or poetry publishers although they would check for him. Once this ritual of their daily conversation was over, Juan would nod his satisfaction, and then they could talk about other things— about Vallejo and Lorca, about the fishing, about where they'd been that day and had they seen the monkeys, and were they going to drive up to Jaco perhaps? To Guanacaste? Had they seen the Volcano Poas? But even if they went— he assured them—this was still the most beautiful part of the country. The people were the best here. The rest were money grubbers, dumb Ticos or banditos. Wasn't it so? Wasn't Manuel Antonio the most beautiful in all of Costa Rica? Even the women the most "bonita y simpática"? But today was perhaps the most beautiful day even for Manuel Antonio. And he could tell by their happiness that they knew it too, and in honor of this, he would recite for them his sunset poem.

After the Earthquake

What happened never should have happened. He said as much in the Report. If the hotels had been to code, if they had taken the necessary precautions, if they had listened to him—to his radio programs. Oh, they listened. Everyone in the city listened. He was a popular commentator, the best. But they didn't do. They would shake their heads and say yes, it was so, and go out to the cafés and talk about how right Manuel Siguerra was to warn them against shoddy construction—how right he must be in his predictions of a terremoto within the next five years, not one of the small ones they were used to, but one like a dragon taking a bite out of the earth. Well, it was not enough to be listened to—to be respected . . . and he could see by the devastation . . . how could he describe such a thing . . . how could he, Manuel Siguerra, the poet and spokesman of his country, a man never lost for a quiet, just word—say what was in his heart. The utter desolation of it, the loss not only of four hundred years of European influence, La Sagrada Familia, the Hall of Justice, the Teatro dell'Arte which he helped restore by convincing El Presidente of its sacred role in national life, but before that—the ultimate antiquity—he grimaced at the irony, even the pre-Columbian ruins were in ruins. And not only their greatness but the greatness of the small . . . the little peon café where he took his coffee with the others at sun-up—the open empanada stand with its gay umbrella, the rundown Hotel Splendide, where he had Rosa the whore at seventeen and his initiation into it, and the disease she gave him on his eighteenth birthday a year later and feeling he was muy macho, master of his world.

No, it should never have happened. And they couldn't report it out because the lines were down, and being so high up and with calamity all along the coast—not many could get in until later. He listened to the unceasing wails of grief and sirens, the occasional explosions of gas lines. Yes, this was the inferno to him. And he had known it and he had not heeded his own advice either . . . so how could he blame the others . . . How could HE, Manuel Siguerra blame his compatriots for their indolence or impotence, when he was the most impotent of all . . . because he knew and did nothing, because he let Theresa and his family and his grand-children remain under the shadow of the big American hotel in the grand casa he insisted they had to have—and now Theresa was dead, and his firstborn son dead with her, and the rest would never forgive him. And if they forgave him, then he would never forgive himself.

So he wrote the report knowing he was damned to hell forever, and like a man who wishing to be of service one last time, though he knew it would never balance out—took out from the first drawer of his desk his father's inlaid pistola with the mother-of-pearl initialing and its fine craft and what his father had given him when he—the old man—knew he was dying, for the eldest son—and what he could now never give to his own because he lay beneath the rubble of the casa . . . and so he made a note that it should go to Armando, the second boy by right of primogeniture—and this was no man, his Armando, but a manicured sissy and a useless habitué of the bars in that section of the city he'd only once passed through, and which he had found out had come through virtually intact . . . and surely that was a sign that the devil ran the show.

A last walk around the remains of his city. His city! For fifty years he thought of it as *his* city—even the five spent in America—even as a representative of the whole nation. In his heart it was only this—*his* city. A conceit, an arrogance, Manuel Siguerra and HIS City. As it had been HIS Theresa through all his peccadillos and his times away from her and his intolerance of her affections. He had been a cold husband—he could see that now. Civilized, kind, responsible, but he had never given her much warmth. That warmth he only gave Manuelito, and maybe at seventeen, Rosa, because she was the first and he was in love with her despite himself. And then he had done so well his talent protected him, his work drew around him . . . like the house drew around Theresa and Manuelito and yesterday suffocated them.

It was bright and cool, the sun caught on the dust still rising from the rubble. He walked the six blocks from the radio station to where his casa had stood, and saw lying next to the stairs, pieces of things—the old headboard, parts of a radio, lampshades, a Spanish bowl as big as a Chinese ginger jar in a hundred bits of red and orange and green. A glint of blue beside the broken crockery. A sapphire ring. He picked it up. Not Theresa's. He had never given Theresa sapphires. He considered them cheap. For her it was the occasional diamond or emerald pendant. Tasteful, and telling more about him, and his pose of generosity, than her own tastes. What a hypocrite, he'd been, to give his wife pendants so that his colleagues might think of him—a good and loving husband.

But this ring came from the house. And yet it couldn't have been Theresa's. He examined the stone in the light—held it up. Poor quality, a carat and a half of poor quality. And looked closer seeing it was inscribed inside. "Theresa/beloved/Philippo/forever." Incredible! He didn't believe it. Some peculiar coincidence. He never knew a Philippo. She had married him at twenty-five—old for a virgin—she had not been a virgin—no, she had lied to him and he had accepted the story, a common occurrence amongst athletic women—he was an educated man, he wasn't suspicious . . . twenty-nine years of marriage and she had lied to him . . . someone had loved her and found her beautiful . . . though she had never been beautiful to him . . . not to Manuel Siguerra who married her for all the right reasons . . . social position and her kindness and piety, and perhaps—yes— because she seemed a little unhappy and that was a good thing in a wife. No frills, no frivolousness that would drive him to jealousy. Yes, he could barely believe he was convinced of it. His beloved Theresa, whom he felt he killed because of the casa and the terremoto—had had someone she loved— she really loved—and she'd never loved him then . . . though he knew—the logical side of him knew—he was being irrational. But he couldn't get it out of his mind and went to see if any of the cafés left standing were open.

Over some strong Pisco in a café left intact near the cathedral, he watched the parade of death go on. He listened to the conversations at the bar, observed how crowded it was, as if there were little else to do with a catastrophe of this magnitude but sit, drink Pisco, and look out upon the square where the birds did not come, nor the sounds of the children with their nannys playing the swings, nor the pretty, marriage-aged girls paraded with their uncles and cousins. And all around—the smoldering and desolation. There was so much to do, so much rebuilding, and going on living.

. . . But he knew, he—Manual Siguerra—had learned something. The ring, which was on the table and which he picked up and turned from time to time, and looked close with his reading glasses on, at the inscription, again and again . . . he knew . . . because of this . . . because of Theresa, of her lie to him—of the lie of his marriage, his honor. He knew he would not go back to the radio station, pick up his father's inlaid pistola, write the final letter of disposition and give his final broadcast, then turn it on himself.

Instead, he would help to rebuild his city. And he had Theresa to thank for that.

Speonk and Beyond

Friday night, the 8:32 bound for Babylon " . . .
Change there for Quogue, Speonk and beyond. Track 16—
Southampton, Bridgehampton, East Hampton, Montauk . . ."
has been changed. "Repeat—has been changed to track 14,
repeat, all those holding tickets to . . ." *(a two minute litany)*
" . . . change at Jamaica and . . ." *(another litany)* ". . .
change at Babylon—proceed to Gate 14—Move down. Move
down. . . ."
I get this in audio spurts—the speaker system at Penn
Station sounding more like intermittent lightning—a decibel
recipe at war with itself. . . . Oh boy!
Never take the 8:32 on a hot summer night, bound—in
interrupted, change-trains, fashion—for the Hamptons. I did
this thinking the crush would be over on the 6:30 Express;
I honestly believed reasonable union men in blue and white
would walk the aisles—their routes covered with the sounds
of bits of information exchanged, and that reassuring click
of the ticket puncher that slid in and out of their leather
holders affixed to the backs of their belts. In tight blue surge
trousers, these railroad Hermes bent over my memories of
trains taken at odd hours to the sticks (styx?), whizzing past
the periwinkle of cornflowers, Queen Anne's lace, wild pink,
sumac, black-eyed Susan—the train clacking hypnotically between towns with appellations waxing so cutsy you'd think

it was mandatory to dress in gingham. But these little, empty spaces—how marvelous and abundant in the waning solstice light. Gardens out of the rich soot of trains—marijuana threading daisies. Kicked by the stones shot from under those heavy, glancing wheels, these hardy beauties stood the test . . . the wild phlox bent with the blows, only to twist and rise again tinged with ironweed and buttercups. Oh, I thought, these kindly men with plump thighs corseted in their too-tight pants will punch my ticket, and nod patiently if it isn't handy, and I have to dig in my overflowing bag.

Forget that anachronism of the Long Island Line! Forget my childhood on pullmans racing around Horseshoe Curve, and those black sentinels of kindliness to kids—the night porters who carried penny lollypops and accepted tips so graciously your mother wondered if she gave too much.

Dirt opaques the windows sealed shut amidst three abreast and two abreast. The seats are narrow for all but the truly slim. I know the man's knees across from me better than my ex-husband's. I feel with my own, the knobs and twists and matted hair behind his cotton ducks. In my case I sit facing two others with the seats turned around. At first, it'd been just me and a pleasant-faced black woman (less than forty, plumpish, her hair straightened, set and brushed in a soft, short, upward wave away from her high cheekbones). She smiles and goes back to her Danielle Steel paperback. Next comes the man who reminds me of Anthony Perkins twenty years ago. He is serious, thin, wears white shorts (white! on a train!) and an alligator logo top. He is completely self-possessed, and though his knees join the juncture of mine and the black woman's he gives us no acknowledgement. He too is reading a paperback. The size, type of paper, and its darkened color (I can't see the cover) indicate it's a prestige line. I'm dying to know the author (I guess Goethe or Faulkner—could it be Proust? A class by itself for reading on trains). The seat next to me, that is connected to mine with only the suggestion of heightened upholstery to indicate the next depression—is vacant, although not empty. I am foolish enough to be traveling with one piece of parachute luggage (full of toilet paper and towels) which takes up the full allotted space of the second depression.

The tide is rising and we still haven't left Penn Station. Preppies, suburban towny types wearing sports caps and holding cans of Bud, secretaries in their short polyester skirts, their high sling-back heels, foreign tourists . . . (now, this is something new. The reversal—the insurgence of European and Asian tourists to our shores. I feel a moment of embarrassment for the filth and deplorable conditions . . . the cigarette butts, blinking overhead lights—the reek of smoke, sweat, the stench coming from the open doors of unflushed, uncleaned lavatories with their piles of white paper sinking and decomposing on the rancid floor. "Oh!" I want to say, "Oh, don't think this is the American railroad system—take the train from Lamy to the West Coast—take the great lines that scour the Lake region. The East Coast is different, do not judge us by this train!")

The pretty black woman looks up from Danielle Steel. She smiles at me. Her lips are full, pink with a darker interior. We have a bond in this madness. Everything about her speaks ladylike kindnesses and generosity. Her clothes are inexpensive but tasteful. Her shoes, dark blue out of Baker's or Kinney's, have been recently shined. The small cross about her smooth neck indicates spirituality. Her teeth are large and well brushed, her fingernails well shaped but with a colorless gloss. "Ohhhh no, you want me to hold your coffee," she says with an alto meant for *Oh Happy Day* and other such great Southern hymns. I see our attraction immediately. Black and white, we are the best of the South. We are polite and pick up broken glass from the sidewalk. We endeavor to pay our bills, take great pleasure in simple gracious kindness. Her remark is occasioned by the intruder pointing to the extra seat. My eyes roll (no mean trick in contact lenses which have become greased with hot oil in this bad air). Hers dance in reply. We have this guy's number in an instant. A sleaze-bag from Patchogue, a plumbing contractor's assistant who's used his moderately good looks and fast banter to infect with false promises dozens of girls living in two-bedroom clapboards on streets like E. 260th or West Maple. He eyes my bag, country music pouring from his earpiece out of the dime-sized headset. What a schlemiel. Boozed up, too. "Here, lemme help you with that bag, li'le lady." I am three inches taller than him.

Oh no. Black woman and I look at each other over our lids. Tony Perkins Proust reads on, although now his knees know the redneck from Patchogue.

"Where yah goin' dere." Redneck gives me a fast lean.

"East Hampton."

"Oh yah. Better have a car."

"I do."

"I guessed you was goin' out there."

"Right."

"Guess where I'm goin'."

"Southampton?"

"Nah. Me? Patchogue. But you look like you're goin' all the way, I mean by your suitcase an like that." What Redneck means is the look of me, and the fact I am attempting to write upside down left-handed (my dyslexia comes out in crowds) in a journal.

"Wanna cigarette?"

"Thanks I've got some. . . ."

"Gotta a house out dere do yuh?"

"A share of a summer rental."

Black woman and I exchange more glances. It is unsafe in this crowd to tell this guy to stick it. I scribble madly in my journal. He introduces himself, says he'll get me a beer if he can squeeze to the next car. I pray for Patchogue, but we're barely through the tunnel. Proust turns the page. Red-neck has Irish blue eyes and ruddy cheeks. His hair is straight, greasy, and flecked with gold. His shirt is purposefully tight at the sleeve, accentuating his biceps . . . the kind of guy who'd tuck his cigarettes in there. I am politely unresponding to the beer, now into Cheever which I think appropriate reading on trains out of New York.

I look around. A nightmare. In the space between sliding doors stand the worst excesses of my Anglo-Saxon heritage. Joe College revisited (boola boola, but without the raccoon coat . . . instead it's red suspenders, a straw boater, bowtie, and a portable bar out of which he's extracted a shaker and is pouring into four surrounding plastic cups what he describes as Burgesses perfect martini). "Oh this is marvelous. This is really marvelous," chirps debutante number one—number one because she's the tallest and clearly the best-looking. Her hair has that long straight youthful Candice Bergen hang to it, and she's in jeans and a Harvard t-shirt over which are perfectly matched pink pearls, ditto the ears, and a Piaget watch. (Mother said three pieces of jewelry max, any more would be tacky.) Others standing join in the fun. Someone's brought a thermos of manhattans. Blue arrow shirts and madras bermudas over great tan physiques, jockish bigness. Glowing with health, they light the train's ugliness like Hitlerian show-offs. Their talk is loud—concerning drink, stamina, parties. The women laugh and play with their watches. The men court the women with their aggressive, jocular indifference. Adidas, Reeboks, and sockless brown loafers on their wonderful slim feet.

Redneck has settled down, thank God. Black woman's back in Danielle Steele. I'm still angling for a peak at Tony Perkins Proust's prestige paperback. We have made Jamaica. A hefty Puerto Rican mother of three tots tries standing with two of them sitting on her. She falls back in the seat. The youngest has an accident . . . the smell is a dead giveaway. Candace Bergen mutters, "Oh grossss, Arthur, gross."

The aisle has become a river of skin—an undulating flesh tide. They stand and sway, hip to hip. The ticket-taker moves through, the address system goes on . . . "Hey now, if you'll settle down, IF YOU'LL BE QUIET A MOMENT, passengers going to Quog, Speonk, South Hampton College, Southampton (etc. etc.) will change at Babylon, this is an express to Babylon, there will be no local stops. . . . All those going to Ocean Beach, change at Jamaica . . . I REPEAT. . . ." The ticket-taker smiles at the voice over the speaker—it's frustration. "A new guy," he tells the fireman from Speonk. "Well, if he can survive this, he can survive anything." The sounds of punching tickets, "change at Babylon, change at Babylon" . . . the crowds beginning to stand up, then sit as the train keeps its fast side-to-side pace, and you have to spread your legs to balance . . . and there's no room to spread your legs.

"Ohh mannn, this is an express?"

Poor devil. Redneck comes out of his country-western stupor, takes Tammy Wynette off his earlobes. We are treated to "Stand by Your Man" emanating from his crotch.

All four of us smoke our filthy cigarettes at the same time in our little broom closet of a seating arrangement. It is difficult to tamp them out without hitting the ankle of your neighbor.

A majestic lurch and grind as the train pulls into Babylon. The aisle briefly turns into a massive curl upon itself. I think of Diamond Head and surf. Again, we—who are sitting—stand. My eyes are killing me. Black woman smiles. I smile back. She has kept her poise (read ten pages), as crisp as Sunday morning. "Good luck maam," is my parting statement. "You all have a good weekend," her reply.

Mashed through the doors, I get Proust at gut level with my luggage. "Sorry, sorry." He smiles, "Eet ees unavoideeebell." Great smile, French, and the paperback turns out to be a biography of Shirley MacLaine . . . the swollen tsunami wave of us is borne across the platform to another open train—the connection. A mad scramble for the best seats from the Southampton cotillion. . . . "Let's see if we can make a bank of seats in smoking . . . come ONNN, Charlie, hurry." I think of Fitzgerald and wonder what the hell he saw in these wasteful offspring and know I am lying to myself. They are glorious in their cruelty, parting the Red Sea of the middle class who move aside as if they themselves were dreaming of them that moment—the green lawns and Perrier Jouet, and sweet sex behind the formal English rose garden. Good God.

I get on the wrong car. I am a smoker alas, but this is no story about the evils of nicotine and our nation's current maniacal campaign. A class system has been introduced in the last five years, however . . . smokers deserve what they get . . . smokers are weak, dirty folk, unruly in their habits, bad in their breath . . . shameful in their moral turpitude. "Smoking section?" eyebrows up, I ask. This is a clean car. It is brighter. The windows, not so stained. "That way," the answer holds a cattle prod. I must move against the incoming flow.

"Excuse me, pardon me, oh sorry. . . ."

"Get off the car, lady, do it that way."

"I can't." I'm facing a legion of healthy non-smoking standers. They shake their heads together. I looked all right when first they glanced at me. Now that it's been established I wish the smoking section, they avert their eyes for the pity of an Untouchable.

Two cars up, my bag which I'd taken to carrying on my head (after all, the bulk was only cheap toilet paper) was now ensconced under the next seat. I find the last of them— a bank of three. A black worker, late twenties—at the window. It is clear why no one wants to share this ample tripartite seat with him. He is dirty, drunk, and snarls, "I gotta friend comin' back." "Hey," I say, "look, there isn't any more seats and this is a threesome." Zip zip. Hostileman turns into black knight, "Hey siddown . . . I'm Gus . . . who you?" a dry, crusty hand proffered. We shake. "Hey, why you so nervous?" You'd think we'd been buddies for ten years. "Too much coffee and the crowds." This was true.

But now I see problems. His friend isn't coming back . . . he is less acceptable and less emotionally stable than Redneck even. Both men are clearly borderline psychos, although Hostileman wants to talk even though he's looking at me with mean eyes, "Where yuh goin'?" "East Hampton." "I'm goin' to . . ." and I didn't catch the name. But the train's in motion, smoother than the earlier train, and he buys a ticket for $3.80. "Here, want one?" He offers a Kent. I decline, offering my Players. He declines. We're at a stand-off. "This train's shee-it," he's elongated the word to suggest adding brother onto it, but of course, in my case, that would be unsuitable.

"You can say that again." I return to Cheever.

"What's that?" He fingers the book, then tweaks my upper arm.

"Cheever."

"Never hearda him."

We both smile. If he'd been a true hostile—if he'd been a black man who seethed with contempt for a white lady and bore this with the dignity of utter indifference (something I've come to know in cabs), it would have been okay. I've played the scenario out before. Rigid silence. "Thank you" and "your welcome" jointly spoken for whatever excuse, simply to show that you were both well brought up. In this case, we were—by the fact of his drunkenness, his poverty (which awakened my soporific sense of decency and concern), my intruding on his space, his efforts at making me comfortable—forced both of us into one of these love-hate stranger relationships. He tries to stay awake so as to put me at my ease. I try to read Cheever to indicate it isn't necessary. Our exchanges are so extra-polite and falsely friendly, we are beginning to hate each other in spite of ourselves. Finally, he nods off, the beer in his hand falling and rolling on the ground. My bag takes most the spill.

I have re-read page 53 of *Bullet Park* three times before realizing I'm eavesdropping on the conversation behind me.

I look around as far as possible without interjecting my head into their space. Two men. Shorts. Thin legs, can't see their faces. One squats in the aisle talking to the other seated directly behind me.

"Well, I knew it was you. Are you going?"

"I don't know. I wasn't popular or anything. . . ."

"No, you kept to yourself."

"I wouldn't mind seeing Trixie and that group. But I haven't any interest in the jocks. I wasn't athletic, and they were definitely the clique to contend with."

"Were they ever. . . ."

". . . and after the ten-year fiasco—what was it—the Moonhaven Motel in Hoboken?"

"Jersey City."

"We were a cheap class."

"I know. Invitations on xeroxes. But you know it was so great seeing Jean."

"Have you seen her lately?"

"God. She's been through what—three husbands? Four? She just got married again."

"She lost one to suicide, then one beat her up, and one left her for her girlfriend. I kinda hate to phone her. I mean, it seems so futile."

"But you know even in high school, she attracted that kind of abuse . . . you know what I mean?"

"Yah, I know what you mean. . . ."

"Like she was standing out in the middle of the street holding her arms out and yelling 'take me for everything I've got' and everybody always did."

"Yah, I know what you mean . . . God, you really were a nerd in high school."

"So were you."

"Yah, I was. Remember Ralph, the quiet one?"

"The one who picked his nose? What's he do?"

"CPA. Makes a good living."

"Yah, I don't know if I'm going to go to the twenty-year. Did Linda call you?"

"Yah. You should go. Really. Go."

"It awakens so much pain."

"But don't you think that's useful?"

"I just don't know anymore. And they can't even send proper written invitations, and what's the dive this time?"

"The Rest Well right near the Holland Tunnel—hey, remember Beth O'Hara?"

"Vaguely. The one with the big boobs?"

"She's a Carmelite nun. One of the kind that takes a vow of silence."

"No kidding. I don't think I'll go."

"Oh God. What have you got to lose?"

"It's the gay thing, but I guess I could give the jocks a wide berth."

"I ignored them last time. Look Jim, we're the ones who've done all right. When you look at the nightmare of. . . ."

"It brings up a lot of bad feelings, Bill. You know that."

"Yes, but don't you think it also makes you feel you're on the right track?"

"I already know I'm on the right track. I've made up for my adolescence. It's masochistic going back to it—oh, by the way—you going to Carl's party?"

"God, he's soooo into drugs."

"How many rooms in that place?"

"Close to thirty. Twenty-four thou a month, would you believe?"

"Well listen, go. We've only got one twenty-year reunion. It's like a rite-de-passage. You'll feel you've missed something."

"I'll think about it."

The man squatting stood up and stretched—and I had my shot at his face. Both are as plain as Ichabod Crane. Both wear thick glasses and have thinning hair. Both have attractive bodies, wear pink shirts, work out. I would say they were in antiques or silk screen. I could see why they were nerds in high school. The squatter inches his way through the throng and I go back to Cheever.

Speonk is coming up. (The conductor announced no stops, now. You have to look fast, and guess, and consult the schedule). The aisle is clear, and I've managed six pages of Cheever—not much of a tally considering the best of an hour has passed, but there have been distractions. Another conversation. Two men and a woman speaking Spanish from the opposite bank. I speak a little, and think this an ideal occasion for a lesson. A close visual inspection reveals well-dressed men—small, in their early forties. Affluent. The faces were a giveaway and the accent. Cozumel. It happens I spent time in Cozumel. Eleven miles off the Yucatan, the type of Spanish has a kind of giggle in the emphasis, a laughing lyricism. . . . Anyway, I do a double take. Mayan. No mistaking the flattened faces, small size, cropped-looking noses. Impossible. Most are relegated to a prejudicial Indian's way of life. They are in service or fish. Unless? Perhaps, drugs? I said, "Hola." Curiosity killed the eavesdropper. They are gracious, fascinated that I guessed they are Cozumelian. I praise the island . . . did they know the tiny ruin in its center, the one tourists are kept in the dark about? . . . indeed they do. Did I like Cozumel? I loved it . . . the green water, the incredible abundance of sea life, the friendly people. In fact, Cozumelians hate outsiders as much as any other xenophobic islanders (my own Florida Keys included). But now the situation being reversed, I want to show bonhomie, American hospitality . . . and they remarked they are dealers in coral and silver, on holiday. But Mayans? It is my first glance at affluent Mayan Indians.

Four seats ahead, the preppy section started. They are well under way, blond hair rests in jockish armpits—more martinis and manhattans miraculously appear. Suspenders, however, was asleep.

. . . As was Hostileman, leaning akimbo across the double

depression constituting our full-empty seat, his paint-speckled hair on my shoulder . . . "Sir? Sir?" I whisper. But he is not to become conscious, and I move myself and my bag to an empty twosome across the aisle. The Mayans settled back into conversations about a contemporary line of silverworking jewelers and I return to *Bullet Park*. Ten pages speed like the wheels of the train, and I occasionally bring up my head to "Oww Charlie, that is such a devastating gross-up—oh youuu," . . . or bits of Spanish concerning Dr. Alveriz's daughter . . . or the conductor stealing a word (or making time) with a honey of a honey blonde, too young (twenty to his fifty) with such glory-filled conversation-making ploys as "Betchu you're the best lookin' girl in the whole train" . . . "Well, thank youuu, you make my night. Really."

Cheever and the startling twinkle of exurbia through dirty windows occupies my mind. I am content. The contact lenses clear up a bit—soon I'll be out of this mire—I'll be with civilized folk, my two housemates, two poets, hard-working, directed, gentle men. We will discuss eateries in the Hamptons, damn with faint praise a book or two, address ourselves to the human condition, put each other's sheets into the dryer. Soon this nightmare of crowding, smell, and sad remembrances of the great train rides of my youth will be at an end. I read *Bullet Park* into a peaceful calm.

"Well, here's Speonk. Oh my, I hope she didn't get off at the wrong station."

The man in the seat ahead of me has turned around. He has bedroom eyes, a fat face, weak chin, split teeth, grayish hair, a pin stripe tie, and a tongue that flicks out in serpentine fashion. Oh no. Spare me.

"Heading out to the Hamptons, are you?"

"Yes."

"Whereabouts?"

"East."

"Myself also. God, this commuting is something else, isn't it."

His smile reminds me of someone I know in Lime Key, now doing time for manslaughter.

"You commute also?"

"I guess you could say that." Now I'm hip to the intrusion. I'm leery of any more confrontation. Can't this middle-management type see I'm reading Cheever?

"Say, mind if I join you? I'm John Babcock."

"Uh. . . ."

"Oh, just say so if I'm interrupting you. . . ." He looks so sincere I weaken.

Perhaps he's troubled in business and just needs the proximity of another.

"No. Please—"

"Great." He twists his plump, though not unattractive frame around the aisle with a fair showing of agility. I take a good look. Now he's reminding me of that Tetley Tea guy. A regular koala bear. These types get away with murder (the guy in Lime Key charmed his way down from murder one to manslaughter). He has small, pointed ears. I begin to see the error of my ways.

"Elvira Madigan."

"Who?"

I say my own name loud enough for him to repeat it over and over. I thought he'd get the joke. He doesn't.

"Jesus Christ, what a beautiful name. Is it Scottish?"

"More or less. English."

"I'm Scots English."

It's the American disease. Geneology. Now, he's on to telling me about his wife, who's a successful psychiatrist . . . then, she isn't his wife, she's his lady, . . . then, she isn't actually his lady but . . . well, they have a free and open relationship, . . . how about a drink at Scuff's in East Hampton? I tell him I'm being met. I tell him I have a boyfriend. I tell him I have strong, repressed Sapphic leanings for older women. Nothing deters Mr. Openhanded Friendliness. He extols the virtues of living with a shrink . . . and what does

he do? Guess. He's a headhunter . . . a legal headhunter
. . . you can make 400 grand at that a year now, he nods
happily. For twenty years he owned a bookstore. Why?
Because he loved to read, but you certainly can't make a
good living at it . . . not the way he did it . . . for love.
So then he became a paralegal, and now a headhunter. Life
is good. This is his first summer in the Hamptons with his
lady (sort of) and her girlfriend. I smell a weird scene.
Southampton College. Thank God. Three more stops. Sure
I didn't want a drink at Scuff's? Impossible, I say. Listen,
you're a wonderful listener, he goes on, . . . having told me
that although analytical in type, he's a man of action, and
he's been with this psychiatrist for five years. And although
she's a psychiatrist, she's also a woman of action.

"Aren't you lucky," is all I can think to say.

He asks where my comrades and I are living. The Springs—
my reply, because I have reached that frustrating point with
this stranger where I simply cannot lie or refuse him. I have
always envied others their defense systems against unwanted
intruders—it's my weakest link.

"Oh fantastic, right near us." He too, is in the Springs.
Now he's onto explaining his feelings of inferiority, how he's
perceived differently by different people (I begin to get paranoid), how his lady and his co-workers are all Jewish and
he feels out of it. The problems of being WASP but he
doesn't want to dwell upon it . . . and then dwells upon it
to just past Bridgehampton, and having bummed three of my
cigarettes. Now I see I'm the dupe for his habit (he ran out
of Marlboros at Speonk).

"Great name—Speonk, don't you think? It sounds like
something sexual from Henry Miller." I compliment him on
his creative mind. Cheever is slipping through my fingers. His
dry truths, his eminently accessible landscapes, his sense of
reason within chaos which brings peace to my mind—are
becoming a memory. I feel incipient depression while Head-

hunter talks about us all getting together with his "sort-of lady."

The train is slowing. "We might as well get ready," I say offhand, but imploring within. He reaches for my bag on the upper rack. "Oh, don't bother. . . ."

"Don't be silly. Let me carry it off for you, I'm a strong guy."

The bag full of toilet paper can't weight over four pounds.

"I'm pretty strong myself," I say defensively in one of those smiling outbursts you kill yourself for in the bathroom feeling stomach cramps six hours later . . . when there's nothing to do but read last week's Book Section . . . and instead you compulsively relive all your dumbest remarks.

"I'll bet you are." Headhunter keeps the bag, guiding me ahead of him. We're between cars now, with the cool air feeling like the breath of angels. I should have stood there for the duration.

Hostileman flies past . . . "Oh Jesus, where am I!!" . . . and I realize on a $3.80 ticket he couldn't have meant to go beyond Patchogue. I feel guilty not being more observant, and I say this to Headhunter as the train slows to the last mile. He smiles and says something indicating that he will not exonerate my guilt. Surrounding us and on either side, with both doors open, the hoards of single bar enthusiasts, tennis players, fathers of two, a minister, and a dozen or so under twenty sybarites press for the three-foot square upon which we stand. I straddle the joining . . . a feat which has always made me nervous. Oh, but we were coming in.

We get off the train, Headhunter and me. I don't see my housemates. Brief panic. I had called at Penn Station to tell what time I'd be in. They'd both been napping after an arduous day at the beach. Perhaps they'd forgotten and gone back to sleep? Then what would I do with Headhunter?

Would I be put in a compromising position? Would I be bored to distraction over a drink at Scuff's? Oh pray for me, for my weakness of will—for my slowness of reaction speed.

I shouldn't have come. I'd had a premonition working that day . . . a voice that said, "Don't go to the Hamptons this weekend." I told the voice to stuff it—something I can't do with others and can so easily do with myself.

"Oh, Lewis."

"You made it."

Thank God. The curly-haired man of distinction—that noble Keatsian profile—that delicate virility that has pared down and improved through the years of our acquaintance-ship—appears out of the shadows. I introduce the men, Headhunter says his name since I forget it. . . . On an afterthought he doubles back. We stand ready to get in the car. "Say, give me your number," he says. "I—uh—can't." It's my last defense. "You can't?" his face registers "bitch." "No, uh—see it was just changed today. Lewis doesn't know it, and I'm dyslexic. Man, I can't remember numbers unless I'm there for years."

"Oh . . . oh," he's willing to go along with it . . . "well, look—I'll give you my number, okay?" He scratches it on the back cover of Cheever, so that now, for as long as I re-read *Bullet Park,* this conversation and train ride will be etched into memory.

"Did that woman ever get off at Speonk?" I ask as a parting shot.

"No, she went beyond Speonk, but I don't know where."